**Lowes**

CW00523366

"Nicholas Litchfield's selection of stories, poems, memoirs and interviews is a treasure for readers who enjoy a good dose of humor with their armchair travel." —Mary Donaldson-Evans, author of *Madame Bovary at the Movies* and *Behind the Lines*

"This is the only literary magazine I read these days, and it's always enjoyable. It takes the reader to a wide variety of literary destinations, and makes even a confirmed hermit like me want to get up and go somewhere. Highly recommended." —James Reasoner, *New York Times* bestselling author

"Reading *Lowestoft Chronicle* is like jostling through a sprawling bazaar in Tashkent or Ulaanbaatar, with eyes wide open and wits on high alert. Invigorating, too." —Victor Robert Lee, author of *Performance Anomalies*

"*Lowestoft Chronicle* publishes some of the finest work of travel writing on the Internet today." —Krystal Sierra, *The Review Review* (5-Star Review)

"The much-admired *Lowestoft Chronicle* [is] an eclectic and innovative online journal. Packed into the pages are stories to entice, enthral, and entertain... incisive and enlightening interviews...[and] a tasty blend of pleasing and deftly prepared poems." —Pam Norfolk, *Lancashire Post*

"How did I not know about the *Lowestoft Chronicle*? If you're late to this travel and literary parade as well, check out Nicholas Litchfield's superb online journal specializing in all things to do with travel, literature, and the overlap between these life-nourishing activities."
—James R. Benn, acclaimed author of the Billy Boyle World War II mystery series

"A powerful literary passport—this adventurous anthology is all stamped up with exciting travel-themed writing. With humor, darkness, and charm, its lively prose and poetry will drop you into memorable physical and psychological landscapes. Pack your bags!"
—Joseph Scapellato, acclaimed author of *Big Lonesome* and *The Made-Up Man*

"The literary equivalent of Rick's Café in *Casablanca*, where travelers of all stripes pull up a stool and swap stories at the bar. Handsomely designed and expertly curated, *Lowestoft Chronicle* drives us into the arms of experience."          —Scott Dominic Carpenter, acclaimed author of
*Theory of Remainders*

"In this quarterly, you'll find creative nonfiction, short stories, and a few poems, with a welcome dose of humor in many. Wander around the site and you'll find intriguing stories."                    —Pat Tompkins, Afar.com

"*Lowestoft Chronicle* is contemporary and worldly but with a sepia charm. It's a Baedeker for the vicarious traveler in the age of globalization."
—Ivy Goodman, award-winning author of
*Heart Failure* and *A Chapter from Her Upbringing*

"A solid collection of funny and fine travel-themed stories, poetry, essays and interviews that easily fits in a back pocket or carry-on bag."
— Frank Mundo, Examiner.com

"An impressive collection of travel works that sweeps the reader across the globe. The characters here, though sometimes lost in distant lands and curious customs, never fail to be lost in wonder. Here is your ticket to travel with them, to lose yourself in these pages, to satisfy your inner nomad."
—Dorene O'Brien, award-winning author of
*Voices of the Lost and Found*

"Three attributes of a good literary journal are variety, quality, and the unexpected. *Lowestoft Chronicle* supplies all three."
—Robert Wexelblatt, award-winning author of
*Zublinka Among Women*

"A wonderful collection from a fine literary journal. Fine writing that stirs the imagination, often amuses and always entertains."
—Dietrich Kalteis, acclaimed author of
*Under an Outlaw Moon* and *Zero Avenue*

# AN ADVENTUROUS SPIRIT

Books in the Lowestoft Chronicle Anthology Series

# AN ADVENTUROUS SPIRIT

EDITED BY NICHOLAS LITCHFIELD

FOREWORD BY JAMES B. NICOLA

Lowestoft
Chronicle
Press

# AN ADVENTUROUS SPIRIT

SUBMISSIONS

The editors welcome submissions of poetry and prose. For submission information please visit our website at www.lowestoftchronicle.com or email: submissions@lowestoftchronicle.com

Published by Lowestoft Chronicle Press, Cambridge, Massachusetts www.lowestoftchronicle.com

First edition: October 2022

Cover and book design by Nicholas Litchfield
Logos by Tara Litchfield

ISBN 13: 978-1-7323328-2-9
ISBN 10: 1-7323328-2-7

Library of Congress Control Number: 2022943882

Printed in the United States of America

# CONTENTS

## INTERVIEW

## CREATIVE NON-FICTION

## CONTRIBUTORS |
## COPYRIGHT NOTES |

# The Event of an Adventure—and Vice Versa: Processing a Journey

James B. Nicola

Travel chronicles. How do they work? How do they make us feel that we, too, have taken the trip worth taking?

I suggest that it is not the events of his Grand Tour per se but, rather, Mark Twain's experience and (seemingly guileless, but oh-so-crafty) telling of it that makes *The Innocents Abroad* far more entertaining, illuminating, and memorable than any mere travelogue. Later, in fiction, it is not the plot but the *inner* monologue of Twain's alter-ego (Huck Finn, while looking at the stars—you remember, Jim's asleep?) that becomes the literary event of a century.

Likewise, it is not only Marcel Proust's exquisite diction but also his very process of *remembrance* that makes sipping tea (with madeleine cakes, of course) and spying on forbidden love scenes the literary adventure of a decade.

"Subjective reality," then, is by no means a new thing in literature. "A lie as art," as Robert Mangeot (in this edition) says? Perhaps. But perhaps the art is that of processing a personal *truth*, possibly a higher one, if not a "closer brush" with a universal truth. Not unlike revelation.

——— ✦ ———

Have you noticed lately how just about every novel, poem, play, movie, or musical of today undertakes to create a whole new world with its own universe of aesthetics, mores, theatricality, language, and even logic, markedly unlike any other? The Victorian novel would chronicle some intrepid hero overcoming obstacles of society and circumstance; the Renaissance sonnet was sure to involve an octet, a sestet, and a volta, with a concomitant rhythm of thought. But contemporary literature and art? In our post-post-post-modern era, one might say that "anything goes," even when the "thing" is not in a post-post-post-modern idiom. "Beginning, middle, and end" still serve, but almost all contemporary fiction and drama, for example, deploy a "late point of attack," then let reader or spectator catch up through flashbacks and other non-linear devices.

More than the *who*, *what*, and *when*, then, today's adventures of literature are equally stories of *why* the author is telling us the tale in the first place, which informs, in turn, the *how*: style and structure. The reader's journey may be like that of a carefree stroll or a free fall, a Ferris wheel or a roller-coaster, a train ride or a train wreck. Such is the "Adventurous Spirit" throughout the present *Lowestoft Chronicle* anthology as it takes us around the world and beyond.

———■ ✦ ■———

Sheldon Russell puts it in a nutshell: "all stories are journeys." Through reading, as DeWitt Clinton tells us, we can "board in the evening, arrive/In the afternoon, halfway around our world." Lao Tzu adds: "if/We travel to a place we've only read about,/We'll look forward even more on our way/Back…."

Sometimes it is the mode of transportation that furnishes the key to revelation. The "Last Road Trip" Jeff Burt takes in a cherished '73 Monte Carlo may lead to an unpredictable respect for voodoo, for instance. Meanwhile, Mary Donaldson-Evans's acceptance of a loaner car from a gracious friend in France gives new credence to an age-old adage—with a little adjustment: "The *ride from* hell is paved with the best intentions."

Sometimes the vehicle is a boat, such as the one where Jacqueline Jules can "whisper into the waves"—if one, indeed, can. Her poem's last line lends the final clue to how she does it, why, and what her "Happy Place" is all about.

Sometimes the clue is in the luggage. Rob Dinsmoor's

Great Plains odyssey starts when he realizes he has someone else's bag, which may not be so easy to return. Linda Ankrah-Dove begins by finding a "banana in a corner of [her] suitcase wrapped/between a pair of walking shoes and a big red sweater."

The journey's destination may lie on the edge of the imagination. Jeff Burt's "Darkness, Missouri" might not even be there. Tim Frank's "Hotel" glows "like a manifested jewel" and remains "so close"—but does anyone actually "reach it?" James Gallant takes us to a city that is "a phoenix"—in "concrete," no less. The point of Richard Luftig's "Sometimes Town" may be "to remind us that we are still here,/and how folks…are more important than anything."

Several pieces take us *under* the city, to the Underground of London or the subways of New York; an analogous "moral descent" is particularly evident in Tim Frank's "Three Strikes." Bruce Harris's urban junket to an urban underbelly exploits a literary world of hard-boiled prose, where "the cheap New York City hotel rooms" become "seedier, people nastier, and the pipe-selling business tougher."

In George Moore's "Isle of Mull," where he thinks of "the dead all day//with the calm brewed in single clouds," we may notice "a few slow sculpted sheep//grazing undisturbed on/the new sprouts of their hillsides." Whether his terrain and its creatures are literal or metaphorical—or both—is up to us. For Marc Harshman, in a "border where all will be revealed," a "ghost of a large doe floats/down" his "bank, shimmering/in a confluence of dreams and sirens"…"with no passport to show." Similarly, at his "Truck Stop," Rob Dinsmoor will ask if you saw "something weird come by here?" In an equally eldritch manner, DAH's "Far Beyond, Years Later" appears and then disappears, not unlike Brigadoon—or more to the point, "like a watermark/stamped on memory."

Then again, when Robert Beveridge adumbrates "The glow/from no one place,/anticipated fire ready/to ignite," is he describing a light "Where the Imagination is Lofted a Wee Bit High," as DeWitt Clinton might call it? "How could anyone

13

like" poems that do this, he might ask. Then again, don't "we all chase our freedom in the shadows of the hills and hollows/ along the way to our final, predetermined destination" as per Linda Ankrah-Dove's "Making Sense"?

How authors get where they are going and how they take us there can be as contrasting as night and day. One of this edition's interviewed authors, Abby Frucht, tells us, "I never outline." No wonder "some of the stories" she writes "might be mistaken for poems." Sheldon Russell, though, outlines every chapter ahead of time. But since he writes whodunits, it is only proper and polite to provide a cliff for his readers—and his detective—to hang from.

Catherine Dowling might tell us that even these contrasting literary methods comprise "Two Halves of a Whole": that opposites like "ugliness and beauty interlaced" are intrinsic to the very "nature of things…each giving power to the other."

For Robert Wexelblatt's Chinese hero Hsi-wei, the making of poems is conflated, or at least compared, with the making of straw sandals. Poems, though, are "made by one person," unlike proverbs, which come "from the people."

———— ✦ ————

Can we possibly be dosed with too much literature that underscores our common humanity? Memoirs, essays, and poems that do this make us more empathetic, more humane, don't they? When Catherine Dowling tells us that "Irish people have walked the Trail of Tears to raise money for famine relief in Somalia" and that "Mary Robinson, Ireland's first female president, is an honorary Choctaw chief," I feel not merely heart-warmed but *heartened*—inspired! We also find out what "the Irish," in turn, have done "in gratitude."

We are all One, in fact, not merely descended from a common ancestor but veritable siblings under the sun even today. James Gallant tells us outright that "we Americans, whatever our origins, are New World brothers and sisters" known as "Melungeons."

After all, though experienced or imagined by authors and narrated by their personae, at their best, these "adventures" are really about—are really *for*—us. So that we, too, might be able "to face the world/away from home," as Jacqueline Jules tells us, with a little more resilience, fortitude, and humanity. And hope: At Richard Luftig's "Liar's Table," residents "tell the same stories/about daughters who call us each evening/to see how we are or sons who ask/us to live with them and say they will/be coming to get us sometime soon." More mundanely, travel literature might give us an opportunity to practice our French or, as Robert Mangeot does, "brag" about having "even used some Spanish."

I suppose a case could be made that these adventures take us to a place that is merely "a dream beneath…airy, artsy skies" (to cite Clinton again). Even if but a dream, though, writing and reading—sharing—involves the complementary processes of unveiling and discovering, revealing and realizing: *revelation*. So isn't that literary location "now hallowed" for our having taken the journey *together*? And isn't that, in the end, what travel—and literature—are all about?

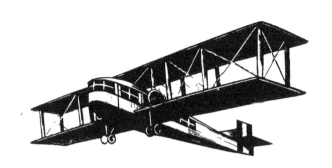

# Enduring Travel Companions
## Nicholas Litchfield

"It's unique and the quality of the writing is amazingly high. Highest praise: it made me want to write short stories again."

**— Luke Rhinehart, internationally bestselling author**

This tenth volume in *Lowestoft Chronicle*'s annual mixed-form anthology series has been a long time in the making—three years, to be exact. In all truthfulness, the COVID-19 pandemic and the escalating health terrors, and those draconian worldwide shutdowns, had little to do with the delay. And I can scotch those rumors that the fat editors were stuck in their palatial beach homes in some distantly exotic hideaway, unable to find a viable way to get the finished files to the printing presses. In fact, far from work-shy, we have been confined to our swivel chairs day in and day out since 2020, savoring the glare of the computer screen and forgoing sightseeing in favor of a busman's holiday.

And yet, the promise of a yearly compendium seems to have fallen by the wayside. Never mind that the resplendent cover was finished in 2019—inevitably, the copy held here, in this reader's unwashed, unsanitized, grubby sausage fingers, has already been marginally tarnished. As for the book's interior, it has been through three complete cycles and might have gone through a fourth had the web editor not moved ("hidden" is more like it!) the liquor cabinet.

The delay, then, is incxcusable. Unacceptable. Malicious, almost.

Fortunately, the quarterly online editions, habitually projected into cyberspace as the schedule dictates, robotically hitting deadlines with the clinical precision of a baby's delivery date, have satisfied the magazine's legions of fans. Somehow, somewhat incredibly, the magazine has survived online for almost a dozen years, and more recently, while the world's population went in search of seclusion, desperate to evade the Coronavirus and test the limits of remote working, our primitive website successfully eluded viruses, worms, Trojans, and bots to fulfill its quest to bring enrichment and literary salvation on a global scale. Being stubbornly small and hardened by Google's cruel, slanted search engine algorithms does have its advantages—our continual inability to appear prominently in search rankings has protected us from malware and other malicious threats.

Of course, a literary magazine can't survive at length without enviable writers contributing meritorious work. Look hard enough in the archives, and you'll notice a serviceable roster of prolific writers and upcoming prize-winners. Brilliant poets like James B. Nicola, the man responsible for astutely interpreting the many works in this collection to the extent that his illuminating foreword might be referred to as a memorable "event," have been propping up the magazine for years, contributing to countless issues and making the LC better than it has a right to be. People know of the magazine and return to the website year after year because of people like him.

Actually, once, long ago, I met a man on a bus in La

Paz who proudly claimed never to have heard of *Lowestoft Chronicle*. He had no knowledge of the magazine's history, didn't need to read it, didn't want to be told about it. He was especially vocal on that last point. Fortunately, it was a very long bus ride, and I was able to explain in exhaustive detail what he had been missing out on all these years. During our heated exchange, I opened his eyes to the wondrously creative and inspiring poetic musings and the sometimes exciting, sometimes philosophical travelogues and travel-inspired tales that form the core of the quarterly issues. I presented sterling examples from the website's archives, regaling him with dozens of stories and poems and managing to compel him to go through the entire latest edition. He read every piece in the issue—occasionally, he read a piece two or three or four times over. He didn't skip a word. I made sure of that! Though bruised and bedraggled, when he exited the bus and staggered down the street, screaming at the top of his lungs, feeling like a mauled Cholita wrestler, I knew he was a better person for the experience.

Our gratifying though bloody scuffle on the bus is a reminder that there may still be one or two of you who have yet to learn the real story of the magazine. The why's and the where's and whatnot, if you will. For the sake of this person, I offer this brief chronicle.

The magazine is inspired by an English seaside town on the Suffolk coast that I regularly visited when I lived in the border county of Norfolk. Arguably, it's home to some of the softest sand in England.

In terms of literary prowess, however…gosh, what a woeful tale. At one time, there were four or five newspapers in the town, but now, only the *Lowestoft Journal* remains. Incidentally, the *Lowestoft Journal* is a weekly tabloid newspaper. Ideally, the *Lowestoft Chronicle* and the *Lowestoft Journal* would benefit by trading names.

In light of the fact that few notable writers or periodicals have emerged from Lowestoft, I wanted to provide the town with its first literary magazine. And so, with Lowestoft in mind, *Lowestoft Chronicle* was born.

September 2009 marks the date the magazine opened to submissions, but it wasn't until March 2010 that the first issue launched. Prolific literary writer Hugh Bernard Fox Jr., one of the founders of the Pushcart Prize, appeared in the inaugural issue. Later issues contain original prose and poetry by, among others, Pushcart Prize-winners Robert Garner McBrearty and Charles Holdefer, Iowa Short Fiction Award-winners Jennine Capó Crucet and Ivy Goodman, and bestselling authors Jay Parini, Franz Wisner, James Reasoner, and Suzanne Brøgger.

Though primarily literary, the magazine has always contained an eclectic mix of fiction, poetry, and creative non-fiction loosely related to travel. And it accommodates a broad variety of literary styles and genres, from science fiction and fantasy, and mystery and crime, to horror and western.

In terms of our anthology series, novelist Luke Rhinehart touted the first anthology as an impetus for inspiring him to want to write short stories again. A reader of the magazine throughout the early years, he always found it "provocative and enjoyable."

Incidentally, he was still writing quality fiction well into his eighties, placing a high-praised novel with the notable publisher Titan Books in 2016. He was also an adept screenwriter—he asked me to critique his screenplay *White Wind, Black Rider*, and I thought it was a wonderfully cinematic version of his book, *Matari*, and in need of no revisions. Regrettably, neither *White Wind, Black Rider* nor his cult novel *The Dice Man* reached the big screen. In the last communication I had with him, he invited my family and me to his home in Canaan, NY, not overly far away from me, but I stupidly didn't take him up on the offer, not wanting to vacation from my beloved computer. Sadly, Luke (real name George Powers Cockcroft) died in November 2020, nine days short of his 88th birthday.

As with his exploratory fiction, he was adventurous in life, too. His regretful account of a perilous boating voyage on stormy seas, with the lives of his young family hanging in the balance, makes one keen to stay on land. It's a reminder that a spirit of adventure can also spawn misery, despair, and humiliation.

*An Adventurous Spirit*, our freshest publication, has that and more. Deviating slightly from past omnibuses, the reader may consider this one a fuller, richer endeavor. On account of having been denied a full quota of travel experiences in recent years, the collection doubles up on prose and poetry, with each writer responsible for a pair of works. For the sake of symmetry, there's also a pair of interviews—one with prize-winning historical fiction writer Sheldon Russell and the other with acclaimed author Abby Frucht, a past winner of the Iowa Short Fiction Award. Here, Russell discusses his novel *A Forgotten Evil*, a relatively recent winner of the prestigious Spur Award, and Frucht talks about her distinguished writing career and early literary influences.

Bruce Harris, author of *Death in the Dugout* and *Sherlock Holmes and Doctor Watson: ABout Type*, once remarked: "Come for the covers, stay for the content. You don't have to be a detective to deduce that the [*Lowestoft Chronicle*] packs a punch." Likewise, his enjoyable 1940s pulp detective stories "Subway Swindle" and "Corncob Caper" pack a wallop. Here, ace pipe salesman Bill Ballentine, a man with top-quality merchandise and big ambitions, finds himself up against tricksters and devious thieves on his eventful business trips to the Big Apple.

Nefarious individuals and dicey situations crop up elsewhere, and often in unusual places—the traumatized subway train driver in "Three Strikes" is far from the conscientious victim one might imagine, while in "Hotel," Tim Frank's joyously wacky second tale, a cab driver and his fare share a psychedelic experience during their disorienting taxi ride. Meanwhile, in "Just Entering Darkness, Missouri," the first of Jeff Burt's brace of absorbing stories featuring a father and son on a coast-to-coast road trip from California to Florida, compassionate roadside assistance lands the pair in a hazardous confrontation with drug runners. Later, they waylay their journey to visit a sick friend who fears his life may be in danger in the disquieting "The Last Road Trip of the Monte Carlo."

The car in question, a bright green 1973 Chevrolet Monte Carlo, carefully preserved by its sole owner and still reliable after decades of heavy use, has one last journey before it changes hands. In sharp contrast, the vividly described jalopy in Mary Donaldson-Evans' wildly funny "Bijou," though treasured by its fusty owner, doesn't traverse the tarmac with quite the same proficiency, ultimately turning a leisurely jaunt across the south of France into a hair-raising adventure. Donaldson-Evans' subsequent tale, "La Tour sans Argent," conveyed with similar wit and wisdom, concerns an embarrassing lesson learned by her son who dared to feast on the gastronomic delights of one of Paris's top gourmet restaurants—on the house.

Elsewhere in France, conceited tourists, oblivious to the disasters around them, amuse and aggravate in the absurdly comic "Practical French Lessons" by James Gallant, and a zealous young American scours Paris on a mission to duel with a legendary pinball wizard in Robert Mangeot's unrivaled mystery "The Montparnasse Moon Shot." The research-rich, vividly drawn pursuit tale, full of romanticism and color and steeped in pinball folklore, is Mangeot's love letter to Paris. The quixotic hero, Tapp Beaufort's relentless journey through dingy cafes and fetid backstreets, yearning for a decisive showdown with his father's nemesis, stirs and captivates all the way to the final passage.

Further murky family connections and the yen to explore one's lineage crop up in "We, the Melungeons," James Gallant's second tale, in which a woman renews relations with a former boyfriend following a tiresome high-school reunion to investigate colorful new details about her ancestry. In "A Long Walk Through Time," set in Ireland, Catherine Dowling delves into the history of The Famine Walk and its Native American affiliations, while in "Two Halves of a Whole" beauty, austerity, and gender history motivate her to embrace her Celtic heritage while at a writer's workshop in the Alaskan wilderness.

Further afield, at an idyllic eco-resort in the picturesque Pacific Northwest corner of Costa Rica, a reptile-fearing printer technician faces his worst fear—a confrontation with a grotesquely large diamond-backed rattlesnake. Mangeot's tense, tongue-in-cheek "No Entiendo" will keep the reader on their toes.

Prolific storyteller Rob Dinsmoor, a habitual contributor to *Lowestoft Chronicle*, has a knack for delightfully offbeat tales. Eerie, out-of-the-ordinary situations color his fiction, as is the case in "Truck Stop," where something other-worldly lurks in a restroom stall. However, a more commonplace scenario is found in "Excess Baggage," where Dinsmoor pushes the notion of chivalrousness to its very limits.

On that note, there's no finer example of the good Samaritan than the fictional Chen Hsi-wei, an itinerant Chinese shoemaker and celebrated peasant-poet of the Sui period. Robert Wexelblatt's superior collection, *Hsi-wei Tales*, comprises twenty-eight short stories focused on the poet's extensive wanderings and positive influence on those he encounters. Blessedly, Wexelblatt has continued to explore the unassuming poet's celebrated life, occasionally publishing new heartwarming installments of Hsi-wei's travels in various literary magazines, including two more stories in *Lowestoft Chronicle*. In the moving "Hsi-wei and the Three Proverbs," the poet explains the title of one of his poems, revealing three provocative stories of vengeance, corruption, and retribution, while "Hsi-wei and the Little Straw Sandals" emphasizes the value of discretion, demonstrating the poet's subtle mastery of verse.

Remarkably, these poems, delicately woven into the narratives, as expertly crafted as comfortable sandals, are as innovative and noteworthy as each of the other poems you will stumble upon in this collection. Expressive, astute, lasting, and feeling as if they belong.

Let *An Adventurous Spirit* seize your imagination and

draw you deep into the unfamiliar on a sweeping journey of discovery. Explore to the final page and then return to the place where you began and start the journey afresh. Savor each piece two or three or four times over, refraining from skipping a word or allowing distractions to mar the experience. And be mindful of whom you sit next to on that long-haul bus journey across state or country borders, or you too might wind up staggering down the street, galvanized by an encyclopedic knowledge of the magazine, and howling uncontrollably at the top of your lungs.

Safe wanderings

# Just Entering Darkness, Missouri
Jeff Burt

The sign said *Entering Darkness*. We looked for a town but found none, thought maybe it was a joke, or perhaps the sign meant a shaded drive with a towering canopy of trees where the sun never reached the earth. There were hardly any trees off the road, and sunshine was plentiful. But there was a crowd by the side of the road looking at a dead pig.

The dead pig had its hind legs stuck in the air, its pinkish rear with the little black tail on top, and its hind legs curled up against the body. The head and shoulders were stuck in the sopping earth near a creek.

"Darndest thing I ever saw," said the owner standing inside the fence, in blue overalls and boots, no shirt. "Never had a pig kill itself while rooting."

"Suffocated?" asked one of the fifteen or so people who had stopped to see what the others had stopped to see. All of us looked over the fence, our cars parked on the grass shoulder of the county road, the shortcut between the Interstate and the State Highway 65 in Missouri.

The farmer shook his head. When new people stopped, he started his story over again, beginning with "darndest thing I ever saw" and finishing with the weather and a long complaint about too much rain some months and not enough in others. I was thinking that a sophisticated farmer would have said "damn" when my son Ben, twenty-six and thin, leaped over the fence and started walking toward the pig. I followed. The farmer followed me.

The pig was muddy white, with several black spots ringed with a light gray. Ben held its tail out straight to see if the curl would straighten out. It didn't, recoiling like a spring.

"It's a Bethlehem Pied Pig, or a Bethlehem Black Pied, to be specific," the farmer said. "Great out on their own. She's a rare one. Hardly bred anymore. I've got thirty-one of them. Give me more grief than a thousand other pigs. Always poking at the fences. Biting ones they don't like. Now, you see it. Ass over end in a sinkhole of mud. They say the pig is smarter than a dog, but not this pig. Bethlehem. No pigs at Bethlehem in the manger. Didn't see the star in the sky. Didn't hear no angels. Had their heads stuck in the mud."

"You need help pulling her out?" I asked.

"Naw. Let her be. There's more folks coming by all the time, and my grandkids want to take pictures when they come, so just let her be. This'll make the papers. Maybe one of the kids standing next to the sorry pig. It's an opportunity. You've got to find the bright side in something like this."

"Where'ya from?" the farmer asked. "My name's Stutz, short for Stutzenmiller. Not the name my granddaddy was born with, but the one he acquired in the U.S. Like some pickled eggs?"

Ben laughed, and told them we were on a coast-to-coast trip, California to Florida to Montana and back to California.

"You've never had pickled eggs? Come on up to the house. I've got a bunch of pickled things. Other'n this pig upside down, I'm locally famous for pickling."

We slogged through the soggy lowland and then up a thick rise to his driveway, and followed him to a little unpainted shed attached to the barn, which housed old farm tractors and no stanchions. The tractors, red, green, and yellow, looked brilliant, reflective.

"See here, pickled eggs, the small ones from chickens, the large ones from a goose. No one does pickled goose eggs but me. The goose eggs you can't take down with a single swallow like a hen's egg, though. They squish. But they taste darker, more alive, so to speak."

I examined one large jar of goose pickles, expecting the brine to be the color of urine, but if it was urine, the dark brown belied some type of illness.

"Then over here, I've got some pig snouts, rough, but kind of fun to tear at and chomp down. Like beef jerky in vinegar, but even tougher than that. I give one to my Lab once in a while, but he gets the shits from them, and I have to keep him outside for a day or two.

Those jars have the chicken's feet, which I can sell in town at the Chinese Restaurant for a few bucks. They aren't good eatin', and God knows why they fry those things. Must be for the taste of the oil and the chilies because the feet don't taste like anything.

At the back, kind of in the dark, are the pickles, and I've got some big ones in there, large enough that a horse wouldn't have to apologize if you know what I mean. You can't eat those in a few bites, neither, you've got to slice them up like a tomato and then lay them on a sandwich. I've got a few that came out bigger than a burger patty if you can believe it. Imagine that, having a pickle bigger than the burger."

I examined each pickling type, noting the filtered sunshine that started on a slant coming from the small skylight through the jars, some a pale yellow, some a pale green, one jar of chicken's feet a dark green, and then the almost impenetrable jar of goose eggs. The brine had started Ben sneezing, and I felt as aware of my surroundings as if ammonia had been stuffed up my nostrils.

I ran my hand over the tops of the several jars. No dust. Recent.

"Does your wife," I asked, "do the pickling?"

"Good heavens, no. Those jars get pretty heavy, and the sight of a pickled snout or pig's ear, all sold out of those, or the chicken's feet, would have sent her into a hissy fit. No, I pickle all by myself. Knocks me out for days afterward. Smell vinegar coming through every pore. My neighbor Wendell says it's worse than the Agent Orange he'd smell in Viet Nam."

He chuckled at the thought, put two hands on the broad wooden table in front of him, and shook his head side to side like a horse might, showing his pleasure.

"Besides, the misses passed a year after I started pickling, so I've ramped it up all by myself. Fun hobby. Heavy one, too. Taking those jars in and out of my pickup wears my back worse than pulling a pig out of the mud.

Pickling's more of an art than an effort, though," the farmer went on. "Doing a salt brine is pretty easy, but vinegar's a whole different animal if you know what a mean. An apple cider vinegar, even with the sugar, I throw at common eggs if I know the eggs'll be eaten in a month or so. Plain old ordinary white vinegar's the best for almost anything, but throw in a little white wine vinegar in something with a short shelf life," he smacked his lips, "and you've got a pig's ear that's as good as any German potato salad.

I like to throw in a little clove and cinnamon, too, and I'll toss a bit of mustard seed into about everything I pickle. It's kind of like being a bakery chef, not knowing exactly how the flour's gonna rise and putting in a little bit here and there to help the process along, and voila! you've got a tasty bread.

Pickling started as a preservative, you know. Ancient India. Standard cucumbers thrown into brine. Then a little vinegar. Now it's more the taste. People like the sour. Kind of wakes them up, and if you're eatin' a pig's ear, you kind of want to know you're all woked up, you know. Wide-eyes and ready. And vinegar will open your eyes, boys."

Ben looked out the door and laughed. "You've got goats, too, and merino sheep. You've got the whole farm, cows, horses, goats, sheep, chickens, geese, and pigs. Do you have rabbits hidden somewhere?"

Stutz's eyes brightened and seem to raise the corners of his lips like you might raise a child's arms to pull him skyward.

"I've got rabbits at the back of the barn. Californian, New Zealand. You start with two and end up with a dozen, the dozen goes to a gross, and then you harvest every month. Sell it for dog food. Beagles love it.

And I've got three llamas over the side of that hill stuck all by their lonesome because they don't get along with anything.

They've got this strange habit, too, of always having their face towards the sun. In the morning, they face east. In the evening, they face west. Like a sunflower."

"Do you need all of these to make a go of the farm?" I asked.

"No. Not at all. The land's paid for. The buildings are paid for. I make most of my money buying and fixing up old farm equipment and selling them. I've got some old tractors that I get paid to show. County fairs, a couple of auctions. But I make good money selling a few here and there to Hollywood for movies. Period pieces. Anywhere from the late 1800s up to about World War II. They'll pay up to ten thousand dollars to rent a tractor that won't be on film for more than a few minutes. I've sold one tractor and combine I bought for scratch money for over fifty thousand dollars so they could send it over a cliff. Real Hollywood, that one. No farmer would drive a combine near a cliff, you know. Makes you wonder who's smarter, those Hollywood computer graphics geniuses or a real farmer."

He opened a jar of pickles and pulled out two as wide and as long and rounder than my forearm. He thunked them with his middle finger, put them back in the jar, then handed the jar to Ben.

"Take those for the road. Keep them cold. Cops will arrest you if you've got an open pickle in your car, make you walk the line, so be careful," he tittered. "I've got to get back to my pig."

Stutz led us out and closed the shed door behind him, then zigged back toward the lowland, while Ben and I walked the gravel driveway to the road, amazed at the people standing at the fence taking pictures of the fallen pig.

———— ✦ ————

Ben, the ardent mapper, felt you learned less about people and places by sticking to the highlights and learned more about commerce, so if you wanted to know the actual feel of geography, the terrain of culture, you had to go off-map. That night we avoided the Lake of the Ozarks as highlighted on the guided tour, with the big bass marking the fishing place where no one can catch a bass.

At four in the morning, we found a level place at a park in a small town. The park had one cannon, one huge oak, and a plaque to the dead veterans in the middle. Dead tired, we put our sleeping bags down and slept.

In Springfield, later that morning, we passed up going to a famous battlefield recommended to us in favor of a bowling alley, off Highway 65, once owned by Sherm Lollar, an old catcher for the Chicago White Sox, at one time considered the homeliest man in baseball. But his bowling alley looked very hip, full of neon lights and flashing lights.

As we cut over another country road to go straight north to hitch up to the caravan of trucks on the Interstate, we saw a small truck with sideboards labeled "Stutz" and a canvas cover lodged diagonally into a small creek bed. The radiator was hissing.

We pulled off, and Ben jumped out and ran over to the truck. Two men lay across the dash unconscious, a little blood, wedged against the seat by the steering wheel and the dash. The bridge they had been aiming to cross had lost the right-side barrier and the buttress support beneath it, with the metal twisted and the wood in spindles below in the creek as if a tornado had blown through. The cab reeked of pickling juice. Three large jars of pickled eggs lay weeping their juice on the floor. Cinnamon and cloves made the pickling more piercing.

The man on the passenger side came to with little prodding, and I helped him to the ground. He only spoke Spanish, so I yelled for Ben to come and care for him. We switched places, arcing around the rear of the truck.

I feared taking out the other man behind the steering wheel, not knowing the extent of his injuries, but he steadily roused and then wanted out. I pushed against the wheel in the opposite direction, and he squeezed through. I tried to have him sit, but he wanted to stand. He had a handgun in his pants, which he took out very slowly, and rather nonchalantly waved at me to move away from the truck. He was a young man, Caucasian, bearded.

Ben came around with the other man, holding him up as he walked.

"What we've got here," the young man said, "is a simple accident. We're both okay and can take it from here. And you two didn't see a thing. Get my point?"

Ben shook his head from side to side. "Your friend is hurt. He should go to the hospital."

"No hospital. You guys get in your car and leave. Now."

"He's hurt," Ben said. "He needs a doctor. You do, too."

"All we care about is that you get help," I said. "It's none of our business if you're running from something."

"Running?" the young man laughed and translated into Spanish, and then both men laughed. The Spanish speaker said something, and then Ben and the two men laughed. I was left out.

"He said they don't run from anyone. They came from Darkness. They never see anyone, and no one sees them."

"I don't get it."

Ben smiled at me as if I were now the son, the little boy. "Smell the vinegar. That's nasal camouflage. They have a load of weed. They're taking it somewhere."

I nodded yes, but an obvious look of panic overtook my face.

"See," the young man said, "that's what I'm fuckin' afraid of." He waved the gun in front of my face. "The young guy here," he said, waving the weapon like a pointer at Ben, "he understands what's going on here, and he ain't shocked. He can roll with it. But you, your face, all judgmental and like, oh my God, what are they doing here, and I don't like that look, see?"

Ben then spoke Spanish again, and the guys laughed, all three of them holding their noses. He talked a little more, and they laughed more. The guy with the gun asked Ben some questions, and Ben answered. Then Ben said one more sentence that included "Stutzenmiller," and both guys laughed very hard.

"We can go, Dad," Ben said, and placed his hands on my shoulders and pushed me forward toward the car.

"Let me drive," he said, and I gave him the keys.

He backed out, drove away slowly, then picked up speed, and we were gone.

"What did you tell them?" I asked.

"I told them you weren't afraid of a gun, been in the service. You'd already died once, so death wasn't a big thing. I told them you wouldn't know marijuana from hay and would prefer smoking hay." He laughed at himself. "I told them you were the kind of guy who ate pickled eggs. A mean hombre."

"What did you say at the end that they laughed at so hard?"

Ben smiled, said nothing. "A lot of farmers grow marijuana here. It's a big cash crop. Keeps a lot of farmers going. Do you really think Stutz kept his farm going on pickles and dead pigs? He sells marijuana. The farmers keep their farms that way. They call it hemp," he said, making quotation marks in the air.

We drove for about ten minutes without a word between us.

"What I told them," Ben said, a smirk of success broadening his smile, "is that we knew Stutz, had spent an afternoon with him, all the pickling and the rabbits. I said we knew the business of Darkness, and now that you knew they were drug runners, I'd have to stop at the first bathroom, or you'd be peeing your pants."

# Excess Baggage

Rob Dinsmoor

At a Union 66 gas station along a desolate stretch of highway in Pittsburgh, Kansas, I used my cell phone to call a man I'd never met in person but whose bag I had. "John, it's Paul. I'm at the Union 66 in the heart of Pittsburgh, right next to the car wash. Do you know where it is?"

"I'll be right down there."

Delivering the goods to a stranger in a place I'd never heard of was the last thing I expected as I was planning to attend my maternal grandmother's 100th birthday party. It was to be held in Bedford, a very small farming community in Southern Iowa. I flew from Logan International Airport in Boston to Kansas City International Airport to meet my sister Margaret, who was flying in from Chicago. Her flight came in four hours after mine, so I busied myself doing yoga poses in a remote corner of the waiting area. Flying always made me tense, and so did my sister. From the way people were listlessly hailing cabs from the curb, I could tell it was a steambath outside.

I wheeled my suitcase to Margaret's arrival gate. When Margaret arrived with a carry-on, we gave each other perfunctory hugs and went to the baggage claim area to get her luggage. After 20 minutes, when all the bags were removed from the belt, hers was not among them.

"I've got a bunch of board reviews to look over. I don't need this!" she complained.

I was happy that this was in no conceivable way my fault. We alerted the baggage department and then took a shuttle to our car rental agency. Outside the airport, the air was like a wet electric blanket—uncomfortable and ready to explode. After Margaret rented the car (sadly, failing to sign me on as a second driver), I loaded three suitcases from the pile on the curb into the trunk, and we took off for Maryville, Missouri, which happened to be the closest town to Bedford that had a decent hotel.

"Not all the grandchildren are going to make it, so we'll make Mom proud," Margaret said.

I didn't respond. Was this what the whole trip was about for her—Mom's approval?

As she drove, Margaret received several emergency phone calls, in which she micromanaged patients' care, and reamed out some hapless medical residents from afar. I felt strangely inadequate: Not only was I not getting emergency phone calls, but I wasn't chewing anyone out. Sometimes I thought my sister became a successful and respected doctor and medical school professor just to make me feel bad.

We got to the hotel, and Margaret popped the trunk. As I was lifting a green suitcase out of the car, Margaret asked, "Wait a minute. Is that yours?"

"No, I thought it was yours."

"My carry-on is right here—and my checked bag never made it—remember?"

We looked at each other in silence as the full gravity of the situation sunk in. "This is just great! We've stolen someone's luggage!" she exclaimed.

"We didn't steal it—it was an accident!"

"Only a Bentley male could pull something like that." It was true that my brother, my father, and I were extremely absent-minded. My father, an archetypal absent-minded professor, attributed his own lapses to ADD, which he said generally only occurred in people with superior intelligence. (When I had such a lapse, Dad attributed it to a basic character flaw.)

"Look, we can call the rental agency and see whether someone's missing a bag."

"I don't have the number."

"What do you mean you don't have the number?" I growled at her. "You rented a car from them!"

"Well, maybe I've got it somewhere. I just mean I'm washing

34

my hands of the whole thing. You deal with the problem! I'm not bailing you out of this!"

"Since when have you bailed me out of anything?" I muttered under my breath.

Mom was reading in the lobby of the Best Western when we checked in. Margaret explained what had happened, being sure to make it clear whose fault it was. "It could have happened to anyone," Mom said. To me, she said, "You look like a deer caught in the headlights!"

"Well, I'm stressed out. I just ruined the weekend!"

"Oh, hogwash."

Once we had checked into our rooms, Margaret jotted down the number of the rental place for me. I called on my cell phone. "Did anyone lose a bag this afternoon? I picked up an extra one by mistake."

"Well, there's a John Shepherd who got here about the same time you did and whose bag is missing. He would be very, very interested in speaking with you," the rental agent said, and gave me his cell phone number. I recognized the San Francisco area code. San Francisco was a nice city, I reflected, and nice people tended to live in it.

"Did he sound irate? " I asked.

"Well, let's just say he sounded very, very concerned."

After I hung up, I took a deep breath and dialed John's number. "Hello?"

"May I speak with John Shepherd?"

"Speaking."

"My name is Paul. I understand your bag is missing."

"Yes, it is!"

"Well, I picked up an extra bag—by accident—at the rental place, and I think it's yours."

"Oh, thank God! I was worried that someone had stolen it!" He was soft-spoken, with an understated Midwest twang. I guessed he probably grew up in Missouri, and lost his accent as he melded into San Francisco professional circles.

"I'm awfully sorry. I want to see about getting it back to

you. Where are you?"

"Columbus, Kansas."

"North or South of Kansas City?"

"South."

"Okay, I'm going to look into the possibility of driving it down to you or getting a messenger or something. Then I'll call you back—okay?"

"Okay. Thank you so much for calling. I just knew it was a mistake—I knew it!"

Mom volunteered to get the road atlas out of her Volvo. She often volunteered to fetch things when she wanted an excuse to go outside and sneak a smoke. Sure enough, when she returned, I could smell tar on her breath. "I need to find Columbus, Kansas," I said. Mom put on her reading glasses and began scouring the map.

"How did he sound?" Margaret asked.

"Concerned but not particularly mad. "

"If it were me, I'd beat the crap out of you!"

Mom found Columbus, Kansas on the map. It was due South of Kansas City, right next to the Oklahoma border. Using the scale, I measured the distance from Maryville and figured it was about a four-hour drive. Oh, Christ! "Looks like we'll have to messenger it to him."

"You're paying for it!" Margaret blurted out.

I immediately checked out the Maryville yellow pages for "Messengers" and "Couriers" and came up empty.

Ideally, I would have made the drive myself, but my name was not on the car rental agreement, meaning that I wasn't covered under its insurance. I would have to drag Margaret along. At first, Margaret suggested we leave the next day at 4 a.m. to get to Columbus at 8 a.m. and return in time for Grandma's birthday party around noon, but I dreaded the thought of getting up so early to ride with my sister, who was sure to be even more cranky than she was now. And then we realized that the car was low on gas and didn't know when the gas stations opened. We agreed on a plan.

I called John. "Hi, John, it's Paul again. How soon do you need your suitcase?"

"As soon as possible."

"Listen, it's my grandmother's hundredth birthday party tomorrow, and it's going to be an eight-hour drive round trip. How would you feel about getting your suitcase tomorrow evening, around five-thirty or six?"

"That'll work. How could I deprive you of your grandmother's hundredth birthday? Actually, I'll be at a family reunion in Pittsburgh. It's almost a half-hour North of Columbus." Bingo! That would save a little driving.

"Sounds perfect! I'll call you if anything changes, and if not, I'll call from the road."

At breakfast the next morning, I joined my mother, aunts, and uncles at breakfast downstairs. We had pretty much taken over the motel. I ordered biscuits with sausage gravy because Mom said it was a local delicacy.

As I took my first sip of coffee, my Uncle Lowell said, "I heard about what happened yesterday. It could have happened to anybody."

I wondered if Mom had coached him to say that.

"Yeah, this afternoon, we have to drive down to the southern tip of Kansas to get him his bag back."

"That's more than most people would do. A lot of people would just throw the bag in the dumpster and be done with it."

"Wouldn't that be crime or vandalism or something?"

"There's no court in the world that would convict you," Uncle Lowell said with a sober face. I always trusted my maternal uncles' judgment when it came to matters of common sense and the rules that most people live by.

"Besides, how could they prove it? There's no evidence," I added with a smirk. "And I don't have any priors on my rap sheet."

"Exactly," he responded with a deadpan face, drinking his coffee and staring out the window.

My biscuits with sausage gravy appeared in front of me. It

was light brown and glistening, with little dark brown specks throughout it. I took a bite.

"The sausage gravy isn't nearly as good as I had expected," Aunt Claire whispered. I decided that it was exactly as good as I had expected.

The "uniform" for the birthday party was chinos and a short-sleeve button-down shirt for guys and sleeveless dresses and brimmed hats for the ladies. Here were the six of her surviving children out of eight, with their spouses, her 30+ grandchildren, and their spouses, and great-grandchildren too numerous to count. It was difficult to tell whether Grandma was stunned to see everyone—or just oblivious. I kissed her on the cheek even though I'm not sure she knew who I was. "None of these people would even be alive if it weren't for you!" I said but didn't know whether she understood me. "It's like you created a small village!"

I drifted around, drinking punch and nibbling on tiny pieces of birthday cake. I asked how everyone was doing. Cousins I didn't know were married or had kids were now divorced and celebrating their kids' graduations.

Sometimes at these gatherings, I would hang out with my father, who was using a walker due to a car accident ten years earlier. He had valiantly persevered through rehab, only to have the titanium rod in his femur break twice and put him back to square one, and now he was perfectly content to have my mother wheel him around all day in a wheelchair. (My sister sometimes described my parents' relationship as co-dependent.) Dad didn't like to engage people he didn't consider intelligent—which included most of my mother's extended family—and didn't like any topics other than politics or psychology. Today, however, I was not in the mood to sit with him because I was trying to stay positive.

My cousin Tracy, whom I used to have a crush on, came by to say she heard what happened and thought it could happen to anyone. I wondered whether Mom had coached her. I was actually relieved when my sister tapped me on the shoulder and said, "We should probably head out now."

We said our goodbyes and got into the car. I called John and left a message. "Hi, John. It's Paul. Hope the family reunion is going well. It's a little after one-thirty, and we should be there within about three and a half hours or so. I'll give you a call from the road. Bye."

For him, I figured it was a little like being stuck on a subway train in New York City. It helped alleviate the frustration and anxiety to know what the problem was and when the train was likely to start moving again.

"That'll give him time to round up some of his cousins from the reunion to help beat the crap out of you," my sister offered.

"Will you cut it out? He sounded perfectly civilized over the phone," I said, conjuring up an image of a mild-mannered yuppie in a polo shirt, chinos, topsiders, and glasses.

"That's because he wants to get his bag back. Once he has his bag, then he'll beat the crap out of you."

Suddenly it occurred to me that there was no way to tell what someone looked like just by hearing his voice on the phone. He could be some huge bruiser with long greasy hair pushed back loosely over his ears, an earring, maybe a nose ring, rotting teeth, a flaming skull tattoo, a bicycle chain for a belt, and the Frisco Chapter Hell's Angels colors on the back of his denim vest—an old denim jacket with the arms cut off with the Bowie knife he kept in a sheath on his calf, right over his steel-tipped boots. I pictured him giving a whistle and his thug cronies coming out of the bushes with tire irons and Louisville sluggers to settle my hash.

The Kansas Interstate was exactly as I remembered it the few times I drove down it. As the highways were flat and straight with very little in the way of trees or buildings, it always seemed as if the car were static, with only the hum of the engine and the rustling of the air to suggest movement. Occasionally a mall would float by in the distance and disappear. I wondered where Holcolm was, the small farming community where two ex-cons murdered an entire family in the 1950s, as immortalized in In Cold Blood. The desolate terrain certainly reminded me of some of the bleak shots in that black and white film.

We got to Pittsburgh and pulled off into the parking lot of a Union 66. I dialed John again and told him where we were. He said he'd be right over.

I opened the passenger's side door. "Where are you going?" Margaret asked.

"I'm going to find a restroom. I'm dying here."

"You're not going anywhere. I'm not going to be here alone when he gets here."

A few minutes later, a car pulled into the parking lot and parked. A thin man about my age in chinos and a polo shirt got out of the car and smiled. "John?" I called out.

"Yeah. Paul?"

"Yeah. I've got your bag." I pulled his suitcase out of the trunk and wheeled it over to him very gently. "Here you go. I'm so sorry."

He shook my hand. "I'm just happy to get my bag back."

He quickly inspected the bag, and his eyes started to narrow. Had I damaged it?

"This isn't my bag, " he said solemnly.

My jaw dropped open, and my head began to spin, much the way it had when I first discovered the extra bag. I stared at him in shock until his façade broke and he started laughing.

"Sorry, I've been waiting all day to say that and see your expression!" he said, whacking me on the shoulder.

My sister cautiously got out of the car. "This is my sister," I said. "I think I owe her a steak dinner for everything I've put her through."

"Well, I've got to get back. Thanks again, and have a great day!"

We took off, my sister watching the rear-view mirror to make sure we weren't being followed. I felt good. I had demonstrated to my sister how civilized people comported themselves and helped maintain or restore John's faith in human nature.

About twenty minutes into the drive, the sky began to

darken into an ominous purple hue. Some very dark thunder clouds moved in, and one of them developed a little dome-shaped growth at the bottom. "Hey, you know what I'm thinking?"

"Yeah, tornados," Margaret said. "I'm keeping my eyes peeled."

"You keep your eyes on the road. I'll look out for funnel clouds."

"Does your cellphone have a camera in it?"

"Yup," I said, pulling it out of my pocket.

The Midwest plains had always been an excellent place to watch lightning unobstructed—and the thunder was always like grenades going off yards away. One thunderbolt shot down out of the sky and separated into a half dozen tendrils that caressed the ground—and crackled like the inside of a bonfire. "Whoa!" we called out in unison, and suddenly we were kids again, watching the fireworks together.

# Banana Baggage
## Linda Ankrah-Dove

I found the banana in a corner of my suitcase wrapped
between a pair of walking shoes and a big red sweater—
or a jumper, as the English say.

That case—lost luggage—had flown across the Pond,
across the midwest plains, across the Rockies and all the way to L.A.
It sat on my doorstep back east in Virginia three days later.

That banana flew six thousand miles in a jumbo's hold to rest
on the floor of baggage claim—who knows how long—
in terminal A or B or maybe D, in one airport or another.

February storms diverted all flights from Chicago. At Dulles, TSA staff,
in uniform but hassled-looking, dispensed with baggage claim inspection
because of the disruptions. Speed over security, presumably.

They did, though, put our bodies through the usual scrutiny.
Shoes, jackets, electronics, keys, all piled on grey plastic trays.
Apples, water bottles tossed into overflowing trash bins.

Our carry-ons and trays shunted through the x-ray tunnels.
*Step aside if you wear a pacemaker, metal in your knees or hips,
or any other place.* Bodies stood aside exposed quite naked.

The rest of us raised our arms as if to wave white flags,
and were patted down and let go to trudge on and on
to terminal A serving local flights and small, damp and cramped.

Loudspeakers croaked repeatedly to say a plane down south
in Lexington had been diverted for our forty-minute flight.
An hour later, we boarded that tiny jet in driving snow.

They de-iced the wings once we were on board and
we waited.                    They de-iced again,
green spray spilling down the grimy window glass.

At last we clambered up through freezing rain and heavy clouds,
up into blue evening skies, westward over the Piedmont plain,
the Blue Ridge range, the familiar Massanutten Peak near home.

Through black clouds a quick descent to the little Shenandoah Airport.
and we landed with a bump blind and braced but safe.
*Be careful stepping down. The stairs are slippery.*

In arrivals, two checked-in bags somersaulted onto the baggage rail.
But not mine. I asked the man in uniform were more to come.
*That's the lot*, he said, not unkindly.

He read my bag receipt issued in Heathrow seventeen hours before.
On a slip of paper he wrote me down an 800 number.
*Call and we'll deliver straight to your front door.*

So how about that banana?

On my doorstep my suitcase landed overnight,
a darkish stain on the bag's soft cover, a shape not unlike
the squished body of a rat flattened on the road.

A mushy mess cuddled the banana, skin smelly,
soft brown flesh like fermented innards—my red sweater.
No one but myself had packed that bag in London

and, personally, I've never much liked bananas.

# Making Sense
Linda Ankrah-Dove

(*pace* Homer and Bob Dylan)

If Penelope, Odysseus's faithful wife,
had succumbed at last
to one of her persistent suitors
and made *love just like a woman*—

and if Telemachus, ready in his wool fleece
to leave the farm and seek his missing father,
had just stayed home on Ithaca
to guard the family treasures
and his mother—

and if Odysseus, returning home at last,
had surprised his Penelope in bed
with the most urgent of the lovers,
he would have yelled at her, "But —
*that ain't me, babe!*

And then, he would have asked the Gods,
*How many roads must a man walk down
before you call him a man?* But the Gods were silent.
So Odysseus shrugged his *Subterranean homesick blues*
off his broad shoulders to wander again
just *like a rolling stone*
over wide, flowered meadows.

He made straight for his favorite Siren
who tempted men to disaster with her alluring music.
This time, though, Odysseus would challenge her.

*Play a song for me, I'm not sleepy,*
*and there's no place I'm going to.*
She kissed his lips with honey-sweet.
But then—*just like a woman*—invited him
to early breakfast with her latest boyfriend.

The hero's soul spilt hot tears at the cheeky triflings
with his manhood by two feisty females in a row.
But then he shrugged again and sighed, *What will be will be,*
*the times they are a'changin'.*

Still obsessed and humbled, he would have needed
proof for *all rainy-day women* that he was indeed a hero,
famous as any pop-star would ever be.
So twice-betrayed Odysseus sailed back
to the murderous straits where
Scylla and Charybdis ever lay in wait.

This time, though, before Scylla could grab his six brave men,
Odysseus wrestled the she-monster to the ground
with deft pankration moves he'd learned in Sparta.
Then he grabbed one of her unhuman heads—
though, patrician as he was, he boxed her only gently
and put her canine nose just a little out of joint.

But with Scylla struggling in his arms, Odysseus's mind
was *blowin' in the wind*. He forgot to heed the waters
where the seething, swirling whirlpool of Charybdis waited.
Too late, he heard her sexy gurgle,
*I want you so bad.*

The monster kicked his ass with one tough, spiky tongue,
spewed salty spit into his eyes. The hero's big body toppled.
Many-jawed Charybdis swallowed him head-first.
Her throat bulged as she gulped down his flesh and bones.
Her growling gut was the last voice Odysseus, the hero,

ever heard. From its depths it sang a rumbling dirge:
*It's all over now, Babe.*

So, if the life-stories of Penelope, Telemachus and Odysseus
had been different, Homer would have had no choice
but to retitle his great epic and find another human hero
to lose his wife, his son, his home, his way along the path.
And then—against all odds—(the bard ever was an optimist),
to triumph over the lesser gods and nature.

Homer would update his epic, a fresh take on a familiar tale.
to ensure it speaks to us today. But the life of modern man is still
like *a shadow that he's chasing on a jingle jangling morning.*
It's a trip to slurp ice-cream one day and get blind drunk on gin the next.
It's a journey that's risky and unpredictable, though
we all chase our freedom in the shadows of the hills and hollows
along the way to our final, predetermined destination.

# Three Strikes
## Tim Frank

It was the end of Mervyn's late shift, and he had just docked his underground train into the depot. He'd driven back and forth from Stratford to Stanmore all evening, the same old routine, every night, five days a week. He heaved his rucksack onto his shoulder and sighed. It had been five years since he had run over and killed his second suicide victim, splattering the poor young man's brains across the tracks. His first victim had jumped in front of his train twelve years ago, and Mervyn could still remember seeing the middle-aged man's tears falling from his cheeks as he leaped before the oncoming front carriage, still carrying his briefcase.

There was a protocol applied for drivers who worked for the London underground known as the Three Strikes rule. It stated that if a train driver kills three people in their career on their route, whether by suicide, accident or murder, said driver would be given indefinite leave. They would get a bonus and pay raise to boot. Yet this opportunity was limited, there were only a few spots available. Mervyn didn't know how many places were still up for grabs, but he had felt under pressure to get his third strike for some time now. He had to find a new victim. He had prepared the groundwork to switch his routes if that is what was needed. Mervyn was fed up, wanted out, and prayed every day for his third victim to come tumbling before his train to release him from the daily grind, shipping ungrateful commuters to their destinations. Little did they know how much he suffered and felt the desire to crash his train into a ball of flames. But it was hard to crash a train, very hard. They have tracks.

The next day he woke up around noon, washed, shaved, and played with his cocker spaniel named Cinnamon for half an hour, letting the dog lick peanut butter he'd spread on his barefoot. Though lately, he felt the dog was going through the motions and would prefer Bovril. He set up his cable to record the football that was showing later in the evening and the dating reality show for pescatarians he was currently obsessed with, both of which he would watch that night alone with a couple of cans of Stella.

Mervyn left his flat and took the underground to an antiseptic conference room in Waterloo where a group of traumatized drivers, all men of varying ages, gathered once a week to discuss their experiences of running over commuters. Most men had only killed one passenger, but there were a few who had notched up two, and you could see it in their eyes. They were the ones who spoke the least as they sat on foldout chairs arranged in a circle, quietly sipping their tea. Mervyn was a quiet one too despite having attended for years, but he listened and listened hard, making sure to take in everything.

"Merv, you haven't shared anything for a while," said Priya Baat, an East Asian woman with a knee-length skirt and John Lennon style spectacles who convened the weekly sessions.

Mervyn looked around the room and felt the strain of everyone staring at him. Finally, he mumbled, "It's been a long time since I experienced my last tragedy and I think I've got a handle on it now. Because of that, I'm thinking of quitting these meetings. But before I leave for good, I was wondering where others in the group suffered their tragedies. I'd like to know so I can avoid those areas in the future."

"Yes, I believe that I understand what you're saying but, and excuse me for being blunt Merv," said Priya, "you've made these exact statements almost every month for the last five years."

"Well this time I mean it," bristled Mervyn. "I don't need this place the way these other men do. I have a strong constitution, and it takes a lot to get me down. But I still need to make sure a catastrophe doesn't happen again, and figuring out the accident hotspots from my fellow victims is the only way I can guarantee that."

"Well, I think you should stay," said a guy with a skinny frame whose all-white clothes swamped him. His trouser leg swayed as he tapped his foot. His name was Gerrard Parmesan.

"I know how difficult it is to get over trauma. All of us have suffered," said Gerrard. "I mean, I've bagged two bodies myself, so I totally empathize with you, Merv. We're all here to support you, Merv, you're special to us."

"The name's Mervyn," he said, "and aren't you new here? I don't need any advice from you or anyone."

"I didn't mean..." said Gerrard. "I'm just saying that..."

"Well, OK, sorry to interrupt guys, but that just about wraps it up for today," said Priya. "Merv, think about what we talked about before you make any rash decisions. See you all next week."

The group piled out of conference room and into The Waterloo Shove, a pub located around the corner, where they propped up the bar and gossiped about what they'd like to do to Priya, despite the fact they found her to be bossy and not really that attractive.

Mervyn avoided this regular pastime and stood across the street waiting for his bus. Gerrard rushed out of the pub, skipped across the road, carefully dodging traffic, and joined Mervyn at the bus stop.

"I feel like we might have got off on the wrong foot," Gerrard said. "Why don't you come and have a drink with me and the guys and we can have a nice chat and get to know each other."

Mervyn spat his gum out onto the pavement and said, "I don't like getting too close to fellow patients. It affects the process. So, I'm sorry if that offends you, but that's the way it is. Hate me if you like."

"Oh, I don't hate you," said Gerrard. "I totally understand, but I really think you should blow off some steam with me and the boys. Everyone's been so helpful and welcoming to me; they're a great bunch. I'm sure if we all put our minds together, we can help."

"Well, I'm very happy for you," Mervyn said, "but I'd rather just be left alone."

Gerrard shrugged, gave Mervyn a jokey salute, and weaved his way back across the road to the pub where one of the men from the group greeted him with an ice-cold pint of Guinness.

Mervyn stepped onto a bus, scanned his oyster card, and took a seat. He unraveled a sheet of paper from his back pocket, and as he tried to read his own handwriting, he squinted and angled his head. He had written notes over the last few years, gathering information about deaths that his fellow therapy patients had endured, in the hope he could divine where the next casualty would occur. That day, before he clocked in to his shift at work, he visited Clapham Junction, Finsbury Park, Leicester Square, and Kilburn. But as he arrived at each station, he was at a loss as to what to do beyond staring into the eyes of random people, city workers, and tourists. But none of this got him any closer to his goal. He was still clueless as to how to predict the next fatality. The only way Mervyn could think of to increase his chances of predicting the next death was to study the experiences of the men in his therapy group in greater detail. Maybe there would be a sign, a pattern, a key. He must be missing something, he mused.

A few months later, Mervyn had still found no new leads, despite attending therapy religiously. He maintained his routine of traveling around London, staring at strangers and making the general public feel distinctly uncomfortable.

As he journeyed from one station to another on a bright but chilly spring afternoon—squirrels scurrying up trees and magpies pecking around the gravel beside the tracks—he got the feeling he was being followed. He tried to shake the impression, but it persisted, so he tested the theory by jumping on and off trains haphazardly until he caught sight of a man in a navy-blue hoodie shadowing his every move. Finally, Mervyn hid in the Newbury Park waiting room and jumped out on the spy who was confused and clueless as to where Mervyn had got to.

"Who are you? What do you want?" demanded Mervyn, as he seized the stranger by the shoulder and swiveled him around until they came face-to-face. It was Gerrard.

"What are you doing here? Why are you following me?" said Mervyn.

"You caught me," smiled Gerrard, "and for what it's worth I'm sorry. But believe me, I have the best intentions. Look, I know what you're up to, and I'm not judging, I've been there myself."

"What exactly is it that you think I'm doing?"

Gerrard leaned in and said in a hushed tone, "You're after the third strike. I'm right, aren't I?"

"Well..." said Mervyn.

"There's no shame in it," said Gerrard. "I mean, we've all considered it at one point or another. It's just one of those things, the reward is so great, and when you hit two strikes, well, you can almost taste it, can't you? In fact, if we put our heads together, we could probably hash out a plan. What do you say?"

"Really, you'd help me?" said Mervyn.

"Sure, why not? I consider you a buddy, Merv," said Gerrard, "I'd be happy to point you in the right direction. We'd make a great team."

"I, er... No, no," said Mervyn, "this is crazy. What am I thinking. Let's just forget this ever happened, OK? Please don't tell anyone. Oh god, this is all too much."

"Calm down, Merv. It's OK. No problem at all," Gerrard said. "But if you change your mind, you know where to find me."

Mervyn gave the group a wide berth for a month, but eventually, he couldn't tear himself away from the place. He missed it, and try as he might he couldn't get his conversation with Gerrard at Newbury Park out of his head. As he entered the therapy room Priya stood and gave him a warm welcome, but the rest of the guys greeted him with icy stares, except for Gerrard who waved at him gaily. Each of the men went through the routine of introducing themselves, as they did in every session, and Mervyn followed suit. He noticed everyone was making notes in pads throughout the meeting, which was unusual as more often than not, it was him who was scribbling away as the others stared into space or jabbered away inanely. After about forty minutes, Gerrard stood and interrupted the meeting. He covered his nose with a tissue and said, "May I please be excused? I seem to have a nosebleed."

"Of course, Gerrard," said Priya. "Take your time."

Thirty seconds later, the fire alarm blasted against everyone's ears. The group panicked, dropped their notepads and darted outside screaming, "Fire! Fire! We're all going to die!"

As they made their escape, one of the men's pads fell at Mervyn's feet. It was opened to a page that had written on it the words: *Tottenham Court Road every week from 3pm.*

As the alarm continued to rattle the premises, Mervyn hung back to investigate the other notepads. Strangely enough, each of the pads had the words *Tottenham Court Road, Tuesday from 3pm* jotted in them in different fonts and colors, except for Anish's—a patient currently on one strike who had been enrolled in the group almost as long as Mervyn. He had written: I want Priya Baat's babies.

Just then, the alarm came to an abrupt halt and Priya ushered the men back into the therapy room.

"Stop crying, Anish," she said. "It must have been a false alarm, some prankster no doubt."

Gerrard came back last with no sign of a bloody nose. He reached over and retrieved his pad, and the session carried on as if nothing had happened.

Filled with suspicion, Mervyn decided he would listen to his instincts and follow the trail to Tottenham Court Road station next Tuesday. He suspected that this could be a potential hotspot that the other men were hiding from him.

Mervyn arrived at 2.30pm—he didn't want to miss a thing. He walked down to the far end of the platform and took a seat by the arrivals board. He watched the crowd as it amassed then poured onto trains every few minutes. He couldn't see anything suspicious, but it was early yet, and he sensed something was up. He had a strong feeling some poor sap was going to fall to their death that day.

A man wrapped up in a black trench coat, wearing silver Top Gun style shades and a Mickey Mouse baseball cap, sidled up to Mervyn and said, "It's going down, and it's going down today. Oh my god, I just can't take it."

Mervyn peered into the man's sunglasses. "Anish?" he said. "What are you doing here? What's going on?"

"Everyone's here," said Anish pointing down the platform at a group of men in trench coats, shades, and baseball caps all huddled around a vending machine slapping the glass to recover a Twix that had got stuck.

"Anish," said Mervyn, "explain yourself."

"Oh, I can't, I can't," Anish said. "Everyone said I'd ruin the plan and I promised I wouldn't. I promised on my life."

Mervyn grabbed Anish by the lapels and drew him close and said, "So help me God if you don't tell me what's going on, I'm going to force-feed you peanuts until your head explodes."

Anish pondered for a moment, then said, "OK, but you didn't hear it from me. The guys want to throw someone under the train today, Gerrard's train, at three. They want him to get his third strike, given how nice he is and all. He really is a great guy, Merv, always buying the guys pints and giving cookery tips. Last night, I used a Lloyd Grossman sauce he recommended, and it was delicious."

The clock had struck three, and the men from the group had gobbled down their Twix and were pacing towards Mervyn and Anish with serious intent.

"I didn't tell him anything," blurted Anish.

"That's because you know nothing," said one of the guys. "We knew if we had told you the plan you would have ruined it."

"Hang on, guys," said Mervyn. "Can you please tell me

what is the plan?"

"You've been caught, Merv," said another guy. "Caught red-handed, lying, cheating, and plotting against us for years, and now the truth is out and boy I'll tell you, we'll have our revenge!"

"What?" said Mervyn. "What the hell are you talking about?"

"We know you've been tracking our movements, pretending you want to avoid suicide hotspots, when in fact you want one of us under your train so you can get your third strike. Well, it's not going to happen, we won't let you get away with it."

"I don't understand," said Mervyn. "Why on earth would you think that?"

"Gerrard has opened our eyes to the truth, and now we're going to reward him with his third strike."

A train approached, and the men converged on Mervyn, lifted him off his feet, and hurled him onto the tracks. He got squished. The driver hit the brakes, and the commuters on and off the train shrieked with horror.

Gerrard stepped out of the front cabin, looked at the mess and tutted. "Such a shame."

The chief train controller soon joined Gerrard and said, "Well I don't know how you did it, Parmesan, but you've got your third strike, and it only took you four years, that's some record. A man with a more suspicious nature might presume you planned it all." The controller puffed his cheeks. "So, did you?"

"Did I what?"

"Plan it."

"What do you think?" Gerrard said tugging nervously at his shirt collar.

"I think it would take one pretty sick mind to orchestrate all of this. Very sick. Because if you did, you'd lose all your benefits and go straight to jail where a nut like you would belong."

"Right."

"Oh, I'm just messing with you, Parmesan," the chief said, giving him a hefty slap on the shoulder. "Enjoy your severance package and use Uber from now on. Damn it. You can afford it. Oh, but wait, how stupid of me to forget, didn't you hear? The three strikes rule has been scrapped. They've upped it to four strikes. And that means you've got one more body to go. Isn't that inconvenient?"

"Yes," said Gerrard, "that is...inconvenient."

The chief started to chuckle. He fell into a crescendo of uncontrollable laughter as men in overalls began to peel Mervyn's body from under the tube. A crowd had gathered. The loudspeaker announced lengthy delays. Everyone flapped open their newspapers. Everyone sighed.

# Subway Swindle
## Bruce Harris

"They were in it together!" I smacked the table. "Look at that," I said, pointing to the photo. "You know what that is?"

Carl, of Carl's Cameras, gave it a cursory glance. "Nope."

"Bird crap. Right there on his coat. Either that or the worst case of dandruff this side of the Hudson. Look at his right shoulder. See it now?"

Carl just spent nearly an hour developing the contact print, and he wanted to be paid. He poured liquid into a separate film tank and gently shook the tank. "Pigeon excrement," he said.

"What?"

"That stain. It's pigeon poop. There are no birds in New York City. That'll be a dollar for the photo."

I ignored him, stared closer at the photograph, at the visible cigar end protruding from the shorter man's pocket. I recognized the cigar band, a Cuban-made Ernesto, retailing at half a sawbuck a smoke. High cotton, as they say down south. Only one New York tobacconist carried Ernestos, a fancy 5th Avenue shop.

I'd taken the photo in the subway of an underground juggler. Two men in conversation with each other were also captured in the picture. They stood next to the performer. One had thick black eyeglass frames and the Ernesto cigar in his pocket. The other exhibited the white-stained splotch on the shoulder of his trench coat, spoiling an otherwise pristine, sartorial appearance.

Carl walked back and forth among three tables, pouring fluids, shaking trays, agitating tanks, opening cameras, removing the negatives. "A dollar, bud."

"I don't have it," I said.

Two hours prior, I sat in a crowded subway car wending my way toward Times Square and a morning appointment at the Broadway Smoke Shop. My first business trip to the big city since winning Albany's 1948 Salesman of the Year honors. I felt like a big shot. I planned to demonstrate the new "Raleigh Dry Smoke" pipe, touted as the smoothest, driest, and sweetest smoke a man could ever experience. My brown leather briefcase packed with salesman samples of the Raleigh and several other pipe brands rubbed against my worn boots. Bulky winter overcoats added to the claustrophobic feeling in the cramped subway car. I glanced out the grimy window. A station-stop streaked by, followed by darkness, the overmatched lighting providing little illumination within the tunnel.

"He fainted!" came a shout from behind me. The man, wearing black-framed glasses, lay snake-like between the standing-room passengers. I stood to get a better look as the train slowed, preparing to stop. It didn't take long. I looked down. My briefcase was gone! Instinctively I reached to my rear pocket. No wallet! I looked back, just in time to see a man running out of the car and onto the platform. I tried but couldn't make my way through the commotion. I pushed and shoved but made it only a few feet before the train started up again. I bent, looked out the window, and watched the man carrying my briefcase walk toward the subway's exit. I saw a white stain on the shoulder of his coat. Looked like bird crap. Isn't that supposed to bring good luck? I turned back toward my seat, now occupied. The man wearing eyeglasses, who had fainted, miraculously recovered, had exited the train from the other end.

A rube in the big city, that's all I was. I cursed myself for being a sucker. I still had my camera. I walked into Carl's Cameras. The thief hadn't taken that. Thankfully, it was in my coat pocket.

"No money, no picture," Carl declared. He tossed the photograph onto a table.

"I'll pay you back as soon as I find my wallet," I promised.

"I'm not running a pawnshop, bud. I've things to do." Carl turned away and continued working.

"Keep the damn thing," I said, ripping the photo in half. "It's torn anyway."

I grabbed the camera and beat it—the $100 in my wallet and my briefcase, gone. Nearly eight million people in the city, and I needed to find two, a pair of conmen. I worked my way toward 5th Avenue. Breckenridge Pipe and Cigar Emporium was nothing like the tobacco shops where I peddled my wares.

I made my way to the Ernesto cigars. "Good cigars," I said. "Have many customers for them?"

The salesman's eyebrows rose. "Beg pardon?"

I reached for my wallet that wasn't there. I felt around, smiled, and plucked a business card from my shirt pocket. "Bill Ballentine, Albany. I'm doing advanced market research for the Ernesto Cigar Company."

The salesman looked from the card to me. "Says here you're in sales, Mr. Ballentine."

"Bill. Call me Bill." I hesitated. "I was in sales, past tense. Haven't received the new cards yet." I waited, still had the man's attention. "So, how many customers for these beauties would you say you have, mister...?" I let the last word hang, hoping for a name.

"Phillips. We record that number and report it to the company, Mr. Ballentine. I really do not think it proper for me to divulge that information."

Phillips looked up. A large smile creased his face. He extended an arm. He and the customer shook hands. Phillips pointed toward the pipe section. I noticed the letters CS monogrammed on the customer's shirt cuff.

"Dr. Southern. Good to see you," began Phillips. "Here for

a new pipe? We just got in some really nice pieces. Come, let's take a look." Phillips gave me a disgusted sideways glance. He was finished with me.

The rotund Dr. Southern nodded. The two walked over to a well-lit floor display. The strained buttons on the doctor's vest looked ready to pop off in machine gun-like rapidity. I sauntered over. The good doctor placed his black doctor's bag down and examined some finely grained briars.

"I could use a book and a good pipe tonight," Southern said.

"Tough day?" Phillips asked. "You don't look yourself."

The doctor pulled out reading glasses and rested them on the tip of his nose. He brought a long, slender straight-stemmed pipe nearer to his eyes for closer examination. In my professional opinion, the pipe didn't fit his face. "I'll say. I'm transporting Sux to the hospital. Nerve-racking."

"What is that?" Phillips asked, feigning interest.

"Sux is short for Succinylcholine. The labs are in the midst of doing clinical trials on the drug. Under the wrong use, it's a death sentence. Sux causes paralysis." Satisfied with the pipe, he added, "I'll take it. What else do you have that's new?"

Phillips said something, but I didn't hear him. My eyes focused on the doctor's black bag.

"Just a minute!" yelled the guard. "You can't just come in here and—"

Everyone looked up. Black eyeglass-frame-man, the subway train fainter, waved a twenty-dollar bill, no doubt my twenty-dollar bill, shouting, "Four Ernestos! Can I get some service around here?"

I asked myself how someone could have such a luck swing in one day. First, my briefcase and wallet are stolen, then one half of the team that stole them practically walks into my hands. I checked my shoulders to see if maybe a bird dumped a gift on me.

From a back room emerged another salesman. I wondered if he and Phillips coordinated which custom-made suit they'd wear. He held up a hand, displayed manicured, polished fingernails. He addressed the conman. "If you please, sir. I am more than happy to assist you. There is no need for shouting."

I needed to act fast. The fainter guy with the black eyeglasses would be gone with the four cigars in a matter of seconds. I grabbed a matchbook off a counter, lit one, and ignited the lacey curtain near the front door.

"Fire!" I screamed, pointing. "Fire! Run for it!"

I watched as the doctor made his way toward the exit. I raced over to his black bag, opened it, and yanked out a hypodermic needle and a small bottle of fluid. I shut the bag and scrambled after the black-eyeglass-frame man. He ran out the door, stuffing the four cigars into his pocket. I told the guard to call the fire department as black eyeglasses crossed the street. I followed him several blocks to Broadway. He vanished down the subway stop's stairway entrance. I kept a safe distance. The platform was crowded with commuters, shoppers, tourists, transit workers, and one cop. To my surprise, a policeman exchanged words with black eyeglasses and then disappeared. "What was that all about?" I wondered. I steadied myself against a graffiti-covered metal support beam when the cop re-emerged, now dressed in street clothes and an overcoat. He met again with black eyeglass man. My eyes keyed in on the copper's trench coat. The same white stain visible on his right shoulder! The cop and the second man in the photo were one and the same! For a flatfoot, he had expensive tastes in clothing! I figured my briefcase was stuffed in a nearby subway locker along with who knows what other stolen merchandise. A number 2 train squealed to a stop. Eyeglasses and Bird Crap got in. I let several people in ahead of me and then boarded the train. It took the duo two stops before beginning their act. I watched eyeglasses collapse and heard, "He fainted!"

Within seconds I knelt down at eyeglass man's side. "I'm a doctor," I shouted. "Give me space." The curious backed up. I tore open faker's shirt, sat on him so he couldn't move, filled the hypodermic, and stabbed his chest. I shot the entire contents into him. If the doctor at Breckenridge Pipe and Cigar Emporium knew what he was talking about, my little friend, looking so comfortable on the floor of a number 2 downtown-bound train, wouldn't be moving a muscle for the rest of his life. I reached into his pocket, took the four Ernesto cigars, and pocketed them. I then felt for a wallet, found it. My wallet! It contained only one twenty-dollar bill. Twenty-percent of my cash recovered. More work to do.

"I've been robbed," a woman screamed in the subway car. "Someone took my purse!"

I got off at the next stop and walked back toward Canal Street. The woman victim located a cop and began filling him in. He listened. I stood to the side, overhearing everything. Several minutes later, the crooked cop joined us. He'd exchanged the stained trench coat for his uniform.

I addressed him. "I was robbed, too. Earlier today." I pulled out two Ernestos. "Cigar?"

His eyes narrowed. "Get lost."

I shrugged, put one cigar away, bit off the end of the other, and lit up. "Nice. Ernestos. Expensive, but worth the money. I know some guys that'd do crazy things to get their mitts on these cigars."

"I told you to beat it."

"Actually, you told me to get lost. There's a difference."

I had his attention. His face had a stupid quizzical expression. He looked like he didn't know if he should stand there, run for it, or slug me. He tried the latter. I ducked; hit him with a right cross.

The punch had little impact. "I'll handle this," he told the other policeman. Then to me, "If you know what's good for you, you'll take my advice and scram," he said, "before you're a very sorry tourist."

"As soon as I get my briefcase and the eighty-dollars stolen from me." I checked his nameplate, added, "Officer T. Rollins." As a third policeman approached, the cop taking the woman's statement escorted her away.

"There's a stiff in one of the subway cars, Rollins. Guess who?" the newly arrived policeman said.

Despite the cold weather, sweat beads formed on Rollins' forehead. He tried ignoring the approaching cop. Rollins flipped a thumb in my direction. "This guy's a nuisance. I'm running him in."

The other officer waved me off. "Forget him. It's Smelling Salts Stan Stanley. Looks like he was in the middle of one of his scams and must of had a heart attack or something. One of the M.E.'s happened to be nearby, and he said Stanley is stiff as a board."

"Any sign of his partner?" I asked.

"This is police business," Rollins scowled.

"So's this!" I placed my boot behind Rollins and shoved him. He dropped like Santa Claus down a greased chimney.

The other officer handcuffed me. Before taking me downtown, I pleaded with him to let me prove that Rollins had been working with Smelling Salts Stan Stanley, aka eyeglasses man. I told him about the photo. He agreed to accompany me back to Carl's Cameras.

"Remember me?" I asked the camera shop owner.

"What he do, officer?" Carl asked the cop.

"Says you got a picture he wants me to see."

"I've got money now...the dollar...and more...for that picture you developed earlier. Where is it?"

Carl disappeared into the back room. He emerged, holding half a photo. "This is what's left of it."

Shocked, I had forgotten that I'd torn the picture in half. "Where's the rest of it?"

Carl shrugged. "Don't know, don't care. I took out the garbage a while back. Might be in that stack."

"Can we look? It's really important."

Carl smiled. "Must be. Earlier today, it wasn't worth a dollar to you. Guess what? Now, it's going cost you ten dollars for this," he said, holding up half the photo. It showed the juggler and Smelling Salts Stanley.

I wanted to simultaneously curse and slug him, but I held my tongue. The handcuffs did the rest. "Okay, ten dollars. I have it. We need to find the rest of the picture."

"Can't. Garbage men collected it already," Carl said with some degree of glee.

The cop looked at the photo half. "That's Stanley, alright. Don't know the juggler next to him."

"He's not part of this," I said.

"Looks like your proof went poof," Carl said. I detected joy in his voice.

The cop walked me out of the store. "We've got to find that garbage truck," I pleaded, "Before the other half of that picture is destroyed."

"You're sure you saw Officer Rollins in that subway car wearing street clothes?"

I looked at the copper. Was this for real? What was his angle? "Sure, I'm sure. I also seen him make like Houdini and change from uniform to fancy duds and back. Why?"

"Hold out your hands." To my surprise, the cop unlocked the cuffs. "My name's Battaglia. I'm with internal affairs." He must have seen the blank look on my face. "We've been wondering why we haven't been able to make an arrest in this subway pickpocket racket. We suspected that maybe one of our own was involved. Unfortunately, that appears to be the case. But your word isn't good enough," the cop said. "We'll need the other half of that picture." He thought for a moment. "We've got to track down that garbage truck. Tell you what, you check the streets south and east of the camera shop, I'll check north and west. We meet back here at this spot in say…" he checked his wristwatch, "…45-minutes."

I hesitated. "Do you guys have lockers or storage at the Broadway subway station?"

"Yeah. Why?" Battaglia asked, his voice heavy with suspicion.

"Because I think that's where our friend Rollins stashed my briefcase. I really need to get it back. Can we meet at the

Broadway station?"

"Sure. We'll check on it following our garbage truck search. I'm warning you, though, don't think of double-crossing me."

It cost me two bits to look through the back of the first garbage truck I came across. After cutting my finger on an empty sardine can, I thanked the driver and asked him where the nearest truck to his might be. For another two bits, he directed me to 28th Street. "Probably see Hal and Ernie there 'bout now. Good luck," the garbage man said. He flipped one of the quarters I'd given him. "And thanks," he said, smiling.

Turns out Hal and Ernie were better businessmen than the first sanitation guy I came across. They pinched me for a buck, each for the privilege of immersing myself in their messy haul. I emerged from the back of their truck grease-stained and stinking like last week's fish. I had coffee grinds in my pockets and potato skin pieces in my ears. What I didn't have was my dignity or the other half of the photo.

Forty-five minutes were up, so I bee-lined back to the Broadway subway station. There was Battaglia, a smile on his face and half a photo in his hand. He took one look at me and held his nose. He said, "You stink!"

"Yeah, well, you would too if you had just spent the last forty-five minutes...say wait...where did you find that?" Battaglia was clean, his uniform still pressed.

His grin widened. "This?" He examined the photo, pulled the other half from his pocket. "Perfect fit." He inspected it more closely. "And what do you know? It's Patrolman Rollins. You were right, bub."

But, where did you--"

"A cop is entitled to his secrets, ya know?"

I took a couple of deep breaths, shook my head. "If it's okay with you, can we go to that storage location and find my briefcase now? Or, do you already have that, too?"

He retrieved the briefcase. We opened it. With Battaglia looking over my shoulder, I went through the pipe stock. Everything was there.

"Nothing's missing," I said, relieved. "All's well that ends well."

"Not so fast," Battaglia said. "I'll see to it Officer Rollins gets his comeuppance, but his partner in crime, Smelling Salts Stanley is dead. You wouldn't happen to know anything about that, would you?"

"I know one thing," I said. His eyebrows rose. "I know pipe salesmen from Albany are entitled to their secrets, too."

# On Reading Too Many of Those Artsy Poems Where the Imagination is Lofted a Wee Bit High

DeWitt Clinton

How could anyone like them, these poems by poets abroad
Written in probably pastels, comfortable clothes, in ink

I would suppose, in one of those nice black notebooks,
Probably a leather cover, with 20# paper that lets the

Fine words sink into the fiber holding every last nuance
& they're always sipping something sweet, aren't they,

In a piazza, or by the plaza, or someplace distinctively
Un-American, something artsy, a place I'm never going

To ever get to, not that I'm not working just as much, maybe
More, but just what is it that keeps their pens gushing on

& on, but if I were to lead such a privileged life myself,
A life of leisure, say, an all expenses sabbatical would suffice,

Why yes, I'd book the next ship out, and probably, just like
You, take up a distinguished residence in some lofty spot

With a view, again, of that awfully nice piazza or plaza
Or at least an olive grove to look out and stare into in to

All that I might imagine.  What is it then that makes these
Poems, well—so "far away" and "art absorbing" with

Heavy doses of terza rima?  Perhaps, and this is a pedestrian
Opinion, but have you noticed that the waiters are seldom tipped,

& for that matter, we never have gotten a very good review
Of any local trattoria, in fact, no indication, not even a nuance,

Whether the greens are fresh and crisp, or have that inky look;
Besides, who gives a rip if some ancient statuary appeals so

Beautifully, so tenderly, taking our very breath away with ahs
Appealing only to the lost who always book their flights home

Weeks if not months later, the relatives having even given up
All hope; or the forlorn, who look this way no matter what scene

Takes them inside themselves for the entire afternoon of lattes.
For these dear souls, they simply cast their eyes on what appears

So dimly lit, as if all scenes like this play better in late afternoon
Of shadows, of whispers heard, of hands moving across the page

In hopes of enlightening all of us back home in Indiana with news
That the Uffizi or the Prado was the only place left for only those

With the deepest passions of which we'll never get to hear about
In the postcard, which by the way, comes postal due from pretty

Italy.  Personally, and if you don't mind, I'd rather book an all day
Tour, picked up right outside the lobby, take in some history, locally,

And I'd be sure to tip the guide who's told this story to those who
Either don't loll around the piazza, or have a short attention span

Regarding what page of culture that could come so pleasantly to
Anyone who could read the local guides.  I'd take in the landscape,

Too, for that's something that will stay deep in the memory, be part
Of something sweet and charming as one lies down to simply die.

But if you don't mind, I'll skip the café au lait or demitasse and just
Keep my mouth shut about how the ambience makes me want to

Drift away on some dreamy cloud poor Shelly has already found.
Pardon my English here but please stop all that whining, sniveling,

Basking in the Mediterranean artsy stuff that makes me want to puke.
But as long as we're here, could we at least make some calls about

Greens fees, as nothing would seem more inspiring than to tee off
Into the splendid natural wilds of a beautifully maintained par 72.

Of course we wouldn't put that into the poem, of course not, too
*Faux pas*, I suppose, but believe me, nothing is prettier, not even

A naked half torso-gesturing god or goddess in some museum
Than a sweet six iron lofting a new Nike so high into the sun we've

All lost sight until we see from out of the clouds a sweet landing,
Soft, onto a perfectly pitched 13th green, & then, an incredible

Left to right slope with a drop into the cup, all arms in exquisite joy:
This place, now hallowed, a dream beneath these airy, artsy skies.

# Sky
## DeWitt Clinton

That's the plan, board in the evening, arrive
In the afternoon, halfway around our world.
It's windy up here, but we'll not feel it as we
Soar in silence all through the night. Maybe
I'll stand so I won't cramp up, or worse, let
A clot or two find their way to my old lungs.
Who'd want that to happen, really?

They come by, the stewardesses, all dressed
The same, saying the same things. Nuts?
Tea, coffee, soda? Would you like a napkin?
Of course, some are offered something stiffer
Behind the curtain, so yes, we're in 2nd class.
Though it's already night, the cities below
Light up all the blue, blue-gray clouds, so
It's a sky full with clouds beyond compare.

I'll make a note of this, just for you, in case
Something we don't want to happen happens.
Then someone tries to change seats. Soon
They arrive, stewards, jackets buttoned.
The passenger then throws her drink, then

I'm in a fine rain shower of cool Chablis Blanc.
Another woman is now dripping mascara.
Others are annoyed, and out come all those
Phones posting the brouhaha everywhere.

The plane shudders, so the stewards and
Stewardesses find their special safe seats.

They close the curtain quickly behind them.
I'm looking into my carry-on for something
Tasty along the way. I open a plastic box,
And finger my way through all the sweetest
Honeydew. I'm slightly chilled in my seat.

Long ago, in ancient China, Lao Tzu wrote if
We travel to a place we've only read about,
We'll look forward even more on our way
Back, a sky full with clouds beyond compare.

# The Montparnasse Moon Shot
Robert Mangeot

Busting in through art deco doors was how I'd come to imagine it. Café Aristarque would have fancy Parisian doors, huge. Over and over, I'd sketched this Rue Daguerre scene: graveyard haze swirled madly around the streetlamps, and I rambled up in a gunslinger's ramble. Except at the get-go, Aristarque had a regular door. Chipped wood veneer, smudged glass, peeling MasterCard sign, same as the meat-and-threes back home on town square.

I twirled my cufflinks, fingered the Camels in my pocket. Aristarque's door was all wrong, but the rest held right: silk suit and tie, full moon coming over Montparnasse. I skidded inside hot, right foot, left foot, plant and hold, showed the crowd my snakeskin boots. But there wasn't much crowd, not near what Pop said herded in to see DeLune play. No party girls, no darkened corner booths, no pinball table. A dozen old-timers in corded sweaters groused watching a soccer match, blue team versus white.

The bartender glanced over my way, and his glance became a squint. "What would you have, my friend?"

English already, a solid break. "I'm Tapp Beaufort. Though folks in Winchester call me Tango Bravo."

"Yes?"

"Yep, Winchester, Tennessee. Over by the Air Force base. Long flight, I tell you what." I held things there, assessed for reaction. Zip, or else somebody was a cool customer. "Make it a Coors."

"No American beer," the bartender said as if a point of pride. His bald head shone as he poured me an Alsatian lager, wherever Alsace was. It tasted decent enough, if warm for serving. Anyway, here I was at last, Café Aristarque. Lair of Loup DeLune.

"He wore black," Pop always started off. It would be Saturday pinball in the garage, me on a pile of *Air Force Times*, Chuck the Labradoodle at my feet, Pop in that bomber's jacket Mom buried him in and talking his usual bangbacks and flip traps. Pop went at his pinball hard, about dry-humping a machine until it broke or tilted. "Hairiest bastard on this green earth. Tall, wiry as fuel cable. It's like he appeared out of the mist from the cemetery way, shoes clack-clack-clacking down Rue Daguerre."

"He did not," I would say.

"I'm dialing you in straight. At the Delannoy, his eyes went the devil's own black, and his body uncoiled, and he writhed like a mad organist at her flippers."

That October, Pop and his buddies took weekend leave in Paris, where the ace pinheads played. Before that night ended, Pop battled Loup DeLune in a match legend among the entire Ramstein AB mechanic corps. Back and forth the game went, on that classic Delannoy *Space Warp Explorer*, leads won and lost in wicked combos and Lazarus saves. DeLune came out the victor, his coup de grace a points-gobbling beast that arced high across the playfield again and again. Slow torture was how Pop told of the ball that did him in, and he'd given it a name.

The Montparnasse Moon Shot.

———— ✦ ————

Ten o'clock at Aristarque. I fished for my Camels. Mom would tear into me if she knew I'd lit up, but DeLune didn't put a ball in play without a Gauloise crooked in his mouth.

"No, no," the bartender said. "Very large fines. Want to smoke? Outside."

"For real?" I said. "It's cold out."

That earned a sympathetic frown but no ashtray. I sipped Alsace lager and said, "Word is you have some fine pinball here. And a fine player. Goes by DeLune."

Double-barreled squint. "Of course. You seek Loup DeLune."

In full-on French, that name rolled out fluid as gargled evil. "I might give him a run."

"There, I am sorry. He does not come for much time."

"Where's your table, though? I heard you had an '83 Delannoy."

The bartender blew out a sigh, that ennui thing Pop warned about. "Better to show you," the guy said. En route to a storeroom, he introduced himself as Michel, and he'd owned Aristarque going on thirty years. He remembered that night and the airmen drunk and hot to challenge the Loup. I explained how Pop kept sharp for a rematch, except he'd had what the doctor termed a major coronary event.

"My greatest sorrow at his passing," Michel said. "He played with much verve."

In the storeroom, Michel unveiled the lady--and a hand-painted 1983 Delannoy *Space Warp Explorer* was all lady--high-class and sleek. Her playfield's alien kick line and astronauts in their NASA buggy were starved for wax. A flipper stuck out like a broken wing.

"A thousand euro to repair," Michel said. "For what? So people lean against it and swipe their phones? Flipper is bad business today."

"This ain't right," I said. Double-shift savings blown on the suit and airfare. A genuine Delannoy in lock-up. "She's solid-state guts. I can fix her up. Not like new, but she'll play a game. All I ask is parts money and help finding the Loup."

Gerard squinted again. The king of squints.

———◆———

I wore myself out the next morning, fetching parts on sneaky low rises in Montparnasse. Nobody at the vintage hardware stores recognized DeLune, not by his handle or the sketch

I showed around, him leaping claws-out from his corner booth. I told everyone to forward Loup tips care of Michel at Café Aristarque. Should anyone happen upon DeLune in the shaggy flesh, they were to growl, "Tango Bravo sends his regards," those words, like that.

Michel helped roll the Delannoy to her place by the jukebox. Plugged in, she gave a whiff of ozone and sang a calliope over her electric hum. I didn't have the bands and circuits to get Saturn kicking, and her broken flipper thrashed late if at all, no matter my tinkering.

I'd grown to understand Pop was ninety-nine percent full of crap. He claimed to have piloted or co-piloted every air vehicle Uncle Sam had, to include the dirigibles and U.F.O.-grade stuff. Pop, a ground pounder's ground pounder. He dotted in bogus acronyms like J-Triple R-Q and HTTP and KATC. That last one was a radio station out of Colorado Springs. But the Moon Shot never changed a bold lick when he got going, never. And now I was testing thumper-bumpers on the Delannoy from his story.

The regulars, Michel's cousins, a bunch of them, latched on to my DeLune sketch taped behind the bar. "Not so tall as you draw," this cousin Gaspard said. "Not such a lion's mane." "Handsome, though," Michel said. "The finest dresser in the arrondissement." Now and then, a regular pointed out what relay or switch needed work, but mostly they carried on in high-speed French over some joke I couldn't catch.

———■ ✦ ■———

Word among Michel's cousin network was a grizzled mystery man of remarkable height and beard haunted the tables at Barbacane, an American-style pub there off Place de la Bastille. "Go," Michel said. "Go, my friend. Find *Le Loup*."

The Bastille. On the Metro ride north, I whispered that over and over, the Bastille, a medieval supermax all *Count of Monte Cristo*. My mind revved and throttled, imagining a street duel in the shadows of a craggy prison, me crouched in that gunslinger stance. Somebody at Barbacane would run out a Delannoy and extension cord, and there we would play, Tango versus Loup.

Atop a fair mountain of Metro steps, I discovered Place de la Bastille didn't have a Bastille anymore. The Parisians tore the castle down to make room for more Paris, restaurants, and apartments, and another traffic circle bustling. Dudes hawked purses off blankets primed for a fast bundle-and-run. Vendors sold flea market watercolors along the sidewalk. Some sweet art, too. Probably they'd had formal training.

Barbacane was right where Michel drew it on his map. Tie, hair, smokes: check, check, and check. I strode inside, gave my snakeskins plant-and-hold. American-style the pub wasn't, with pop music America long forgot about, and vinegar flanking the ketchup. Boar meat ground into sausage. Straight pig, that was American sausage. Barbacane did have serious pinball, these student types working horror movie titles.

I had a sweat and shin splint going, so I grabbed a table and did recon over a lager. Half-starved, I ordered that boar sausage. It came with fries and the fries with mayo, and hell, it tasted pretty good.

When Pop hadn't bragged on top-gunning jets, he bragged on being Ramstein base pinball champ. One day, Pop swore, he'd pull chocks and join the pro circuit, just we watch. The circuit paid five times minimum what Uncle Sam did. New carburetor money always swallowed the travel fund, or else a wrist sprain. Sometimes, he reeled off the wild stuff French people cooked to eat, snouts and tails, bugs, fish every which way, even pickled.

Maybe Pop got the Loup first, but I got him on weird-ass sausage.

I wide-stepped it over to the machines, snakeskins scuffing tile. Then my game did the talking, crushing high score on a zombie apocalypse title, calling out which undead jag-wagon got biffed down next. This student type Véronique watched the massacre. She was off-the-chain exotic, with raven hair highlighted purple. Nashville, she dubbed me—*Nash-veel-luh*—even after I mentioned going by Tango Bravo. She could call me anything, how her accent French-kissed a word.

I followed the student types outside for a smoke, everybody rubbing their arms against the cold. I passed around the DeLune sketch of him creeping furtively through a parlor window.

"Nice," Véronique said. She lifted her head when she dragged on her cigarette, exhaled the same way.

"I'm fixing to whoop on him. On an '83 Delannoy, cream of the fricking cream. Me and him would be throwing down now, except he's like gone to ground."

"To ground," Véronique said.

"My plan is, put him away first ball. Go shock-and-awe before he starts in on me."

Véronique tugged loose the DeLune sketch and stabbed her onyx fingernail on his snout. "You should draw for comic books," she said. "If this gargoyle walks by now, we would run screaming for the gendarmes."

Sure, I amped the hair factor, and his ears spread bat-like, and the teeth gnashed crooked. Over the years, I'd sketched DeLune poised atop a Delannoy or emerging from cemetery mist, always crackling with menace. Pop examined each drawing, requested a tweak or two, and declared, "That's him, boy. That's DeLune."

What Véronique needed was context, so I shared Pop's story and the Loup's ruthless Moon Shot. Then I was telling her about the first game I beat Pop and how he blamed losing on his trick wrist; about his funeral and working in the same tool shop he did.

"Nashville the artist," Véronique said, "and your father the novelist."

———— ✦ ————

One Saturday, I'd asked Pop how come the internet had zero trace of DeLune, him a supposed wizard's wizard. How come Pop took no pictures that night.

"You break red getting photo evidence," Pop said. He scanned the garage, all conspiratorial. "Here's the sitrep. Some of why the crew and me were in the country remains A.F. top classified, K.9. level zulu quatorze. Suffice it to say the Loup don't have no given name that he lets on. No street address."

"You made that up," I said.

"Tango bravo, fox one," Pop hollered and smacked the plunger.

"He's not real," I said.

"Take it from me, boy. He is real enough."

What was real: Pop's cars went through bum carburetors like he did restored machines, and him a certified mechanic. On my Paris map was a mayo stain that earlier, when stared at a while, resembled DeLune in his perma-snarl. Now, it just looked like a stain.

———— ✦ ————

Michel phoned me at the Metro stop. "My friend," he said over TV sports in the background, "important news."

I sniffed at my suit. It was developing an odor, and on top of everything, I'd caught that ennui business. "Sir," I said, "you swore up and down my sketches were DeLune. I got people not even thinking he's human."

"Not human?"

"I own that, drawing him fierce. But I'm wondering why you sent me all over Paris after the boogeyman."

"Yes," Michel said. "Your drawing, this is caricature. Excellent in skill, but the fangs, such claws? No, it is his eyes. You capture their essence to perfection. Near our lady, his eyes turned the abyss that you draw."

DeLune. I'd sketched his eyes in charcoal until their heartless depth simmered the devil's black. Pop's every telling, the devil's own black. I'd tried drawing for comic books. Tried, crashed, and burned. Comic books, graphic design, concert posters. An art school in Georgia nixed me twice off a single application, no apparent reason other than rolling harsh.

"I'm run ragged," I said. "You ever do see DeLune, say Tango left his regards."

"But this is the news I bring! Tonight, Gaspard has a cigarette. A gray-bearded man appears on Rue Daguerre. Lean, this man, well-dressed, a jealous rage when he speaks of our Delannoy. He demands to buy her, for ten thousand Euro in banknotes. Banknotes, friend Tango."

"Bearded?" I said. "Not a goatee or soul patch?"

"Yes, you see it. This man leaves his card with an address in Pointoise. The Musee Flipper Mondial. I slap this bar and cry, 'Gaspard, you meet *Le Loup!*' To Pontoise, my friend. To Pontoise, or you know only regret."

I heard the Delannoy chime a tune. So close, she seemed to sing. So close.

———— ✦ ————

The Metro didn't run as far north as Pontoise. That long a haul went on the RER line, and I missed the next train deciphering the ticket dispensers and platforms. It took forever until I reached Pontoise, its mess of apartment blocks swirled in graffiti. My feet rubbed near raw, I skipped any plant-and-hold into Aux Courtaud.

The hostess claimed to have no idea about werewolves, perky about it, but she said Aux Courtaud was famous for its pinball and chopped steak if I wanted to see for myself.

It was on then, something. The hostess got me a Coke no charge and waved over her matron-looking boss. The owner lady knew full well about that card. For what sounded an overstayed welcome, her brother Rafale DeLune ran his museum from the basement.

Rafale DeLune. A beastly ring. Beastly, yet refined. The

sister described him as silver-templed and throwing away his children's inheritance on a pinball obsession. She pointed none-too-gently at a stairwell sign for the Musee Flipper Mondial with its basement door shuttered for past touring hours.

The sister knocked hard, and poking a head out normal-height was a guy with an urbanite scarf and bristly stubble going.

"Hey," I said.

Rafale ushered me downstairs, along a habitrail taped on the floor. The cellar was jammed with classic-title machines and framed pictures of Paris café high times.

"I'm fixing an '83 *Space Warp Explorer* myself," I said. "But you knew that already."

"An exquisite table."

"Yep, a Space Warp Explorer, all systems go but for a shorted flipper and dead bumper. Saturn."

I braced for anything, a toothy scowl, a war bellow, us grappling hand-to-hand. What happened was Rafale chirped and hustled down the habitrail into a spare room. Around when I wondered if he'd beaten it out the back, he trundled in saying "*Allô*" and carrying a mother lode of spare parts.

"Sir," I said, "let's drop pretenses. Tonight, in Montparnasse, you offered to buy that Delannoy for ten thousand Euro."

"Impossible," he said. "My heart should treasure this title, but I have nothing such Euro to pay. Please, send photos of the finished machine. I display them with honor."

Photos. The Loup's old flame, and he wasn't raving to see her. Rafale was lighting a pipe and checking his tables for dust. That and a museum with signage and tour route seemed overly public for a secretive mist-lurker.

"Sir," I said, "I'm betting you're not Loup DeLune."

Rafale kept sorting his spare parts. "Such a *nom de scène*. Too long since I hear it."

"A nom of what?"

"My cousin Michel, a true man of flipper. Once the semi-pro. I remember he kept a Delannoy at his café."

"Aristarque," I said.

Rafale brightened. "You know it?"

———✦———

Despite the hour, things were going strong when I made it back to Café Aristarque. The regulars celebrated me and my stock parts with a victory round.

I fell onto an open stool. "You had me going," I told Michel.

He poured me a lager. "From tonight, my beer is only ever free for the great Tango."

"Sir, did I piss you off?"

"Sins of the father," Michel said. "Beyond atoned for. Look at our Delannoy! What in Paris shines brighter?"

True that. She sparkled and purred, and her alien dancers kick-lined for the stars, and her astronauts tooled around in their space buggy, everyone having the time of their lives. Last I'd seen a grin like theirs, Pop was laid out in his casket and smiling at the hereafter.

I said, "Did you even play Pop?"

"I tell you this," Michel said. "That night, your father broke my damned machine."

I couldn't decide to laugh or what, so I drank lager and let the *Space Warp Explorer* sing. Come morning, Saturn would be a cosmic hazard again, though her wayward flipper would forever remain lady's choice.

The thing was, it didn't feel like Pop had much sinned. He flamed out hard, but he'd been here. He'd made it another canvas painted over with slick talk and acronyms. Easier than admitting the truth, I guessed. And his crowning glory.

A lie. A lie as art. It got me thinking about the comic book people and what I could submit as a portfolio. A grand bust-in through grand doors. A scooter chase across Paris. The Eiffel Tower flashing and me hot-footing it after Loup DeLune up an iron maze of stairs. Hang gliders. Dungeon hideouts. Guard boar. A showdown at the Louvre courtyard, with flintlocks and everyone dressed to the nines.

The Montparnasse Moon Shot. In my version, I would work in more Véronique.

# Practical French Lessons
## James Gallant

Translate the following passages from English into French.

I

*(Maid Marla has served soup to Madame Mignon and Mr. Cuistance. Cuistance stands at a window as Jacques enters.)*

JACQUES: Please forgive my tardiness. What time is it?

MADAME: It is two forty-six.

JACQUES: To catch a city bus between noon and three in Paris is very difficult. I don't know why.

MADAME: Nor do I. Mr. Cuistance, do you know?

CUISTANCE: (pointing) Extraordinary! A man dressed all in white on the roof over there appears to have wings.

MARLA: It is cloudy. I believe it will rain.

JACQUES: Well, it is April, the month of showers.

CUISTANCE: The wings are transparent. He looks like an angel, or a gigantic albino horsefly (*albinos taon*).

MARLA: April showers bring May flowers.

JACQUES: What is the origin of that commonplace (*banale*).

MADAME: I believe it is a very old saying in the Northern hemisphere.

CUISTANCE: The man is gently flapping his wings, like a moth at rest.

JACQUES: (*whispering to Madame Mignon*): Who is this man?

MADAME: He is Mr. Cuistance.

JACQUES: He is a friend of yours?

MADAME: I have no idea who he is. He joined us as we were having soup.

MARLA: We had tomato soup.

JACQUES: I much prefer chicken noodle soup (*soupe de nouilles au poulet*).

MARLA: I am afraid we do not have any of that. We have

onion soup.

JACQUES: I am not hungry. However, I am very horny (*libineux*).

MARLA: I like to see that in a man.

JACQUES: You will not have to look very far.

MADAM: Is that our phone ringing?

MARLA: No, it is next door. (*la porte à côté*).

MADAME: That phone rings constantly since the new man arrived. We also hear repeatedly a mysterious thud. (*bruit sourd*).

JACQUES: The main cause of my delay was the long line at American Express. I was behind a very brash (*impétueux*) man. He wore luminescent sneakers (*chaussures de sport*). He was probably an American.

MADAME: Be careful what you say, Jacques. Remember, Marla is an American.

JACQUES: How could I forget? American women are the most sexually liberated in the world.

MADAME: You made arrangements for your tour of Provence?

JACQUES: Yes. I leave Monday at noon. I will visit Orange to see the triumphal arch and the Roman theater. Then I will go to Avignon.

CUISTANCE: A giraffe has appeared on the roof beside the winged man!

MADAME: And after Avignon?

JACQUES: I go to Arles.

MADAME: I understand they are showing *Gone with the Wind* at the Roman amphitheater there on summer nights.

JACQUES: A charming coalescence (*fusion*) of the ancient and the modern!

CUISTANCE: The man has risen to the ledge. My God! I believe he will attempt flight!

MADAME: There is that thud again.

MARLA: No, I believe it came from the street that time.

JACQUES: Is that blood Mr. Cuistance is vomiting?

MARLA: I believe it is tomato soup.

# II
## *(The phone rings.)*

PIERRE: Hello, Pierre Clement here.

CLAUDE: Hello, Pierre. This is Claude Martin.

PIERRE: Claude! How are you?

CLAUDE: I am well. And you?

PIERRE: I, too, am well. I know you have been in Italy. When did you come to Paris?

CLAUDE: Yesterday at three-thirty in the afternoon, by air.

PIERRE: You flew first-class?

CLAUDE: No, we had to leave Italy hurriedly. Only economy seats were available.

PIERRE: I am sorry to hear it. I know leg room (*espace pour les jambes*) is slight on economy flights.

CLAUDE: It was just as well (*d'accord*). They would not think to look for me in second-class.

PIERRE: You travel a great deal.

CLAUDE: I tire of it sometimes. So many addresses, and so many different names in different places. I sometimes forget who I am supposed to be.

PIERRE: It is an occupational hazard you must tolerate.

CLAUDE: Yes. I just brokered a deal involving a ton of opium from Afghanistan.

PIERRE: How is Claire?

CLAUDE: She is fine.

PIERRE: Is she still eager for a ménage a trois?

CLAUDE: She speaks of it from time to time. Tonight, she wishes to attend the concert by the guitar virtuoso Andres Segovia at the Théâtre du Châtelet. She asks if you would like to make a threesome.

PIERRE: With pleasure! I have met a charming young woman from Wisconsin in the United States, Elise. She is in Paris studying the French language. Might she join us?

CLAUDE: Yes, of course. The more the merrier! (*Plus nous serons, meilleur ce sera!*)

PIERRE: She is studying, in addition to the French language, the philosophy of Descartes and Malebranche.

CLAUDE: I would not hold it against her.

## III

*(The steamship bearing two American friends has docked at Le Havre.)*

BRUCE: I would like very much to visit Dijon while we are in France.

HENRY: You are interested in mustard?

BRUCE: (laughing) Dijon was, indeed, the mustard capital in the Middle Ages.

HENRY: I would like Dijon, I think, if the color did not always remind me of diarrhea.

BRUCE: When King François the First visited the city of Dijon, he exclaimed, "My god, there are a hundred bell towers!"

HENRY: Do they still exist?

BRUCE: No, our American planes bombed crap (*merde*) out of them during the German occupation.

*(The two friends leave the ship)*

HENRY: I am very nervous about this car I purchased by telephone long-distance from New York. I find it suspicious that the name of the Peugeot representative who is to meet us is Leblanc.

BRUCE: Nonsense. Peugeot has every reason to treat well its international clientele.

That fellow over there jingling the keyring (*porte-clés*) must be your man.

*(The Peugeot representative introduces himself, and leads the two Americans to the parking lot at the port.)*

BRUCE: We saw your beautiful white modern city from the deck of our ship.

LEBLANC: It is made entirely of concrete (*béton*).

HENRY: Why is that?

LEBLANC: After you Americans bombed crap out of us in the

Forties, we rebuilt the city with concrete. It was fast and cheap.

BRUCE: Your city is a phoenix!

LEBLANC: A concrete phoenix...There is your little red Peugeot.

HENRY: Is there anything I should know about the car before I drive it?

LEBLANC: The motor will sound like that of an airplane, but you will get used to it.

HENRY: What is the maximum speed?

LEBLANC: Ninety.

HENRY: We intend to drive to Paris today.

LEBLANC: I cannot recommend driving at anything like maximum speed, because the car will shake as if it would fall apart. Also, there are very sharp curves in the highway between here and Paris.

BRUCE: We are very hungry. Is there a restaurant near the harbor?

LEBLANC: No, but on the road to Paris, you will soon pass a Burger King. You will feel right at home.

BRUCE: Henry and I do not eat beef

LEBLANC: You are expatriates?

*(The two Americans are on the road.)*

BRUCE: Henry, you drive like a little old lady. What is your speed?

HENRY: You didn't see the signs back there for sharp curves ahead?

BRUCE: That driver behind us is very angry. I weary of his honking (*coup de klaxon*). Now he is giving us the finger.

HENRY: *My god!* The fool is going around us! There is a curve directly ahead!

*(A loud crash. The two friends pass a scene of two cars on fire. Trapped passengers are wild-eyed and screaming.)*

HENRY: By the way, Bruce, I forgot to mention that when we stopped at the gas station back there, I telephoned Rouen and reserved a room for us there tonight. If we were to press on to Paris, our arrival would be very late.

BRUCE: That was very smart, Henry—and I have heard Rouen is very picturesque.

HENRY: It was the setting for many of the stories of Maupassant,

BRUCE: I apologize for my remarks about your driving. They were unwarranted.

HENRY: Apology accepted. It occurs to me that driving is the one thing in this world we have never done together.

BRUCE: (nodding) We must be careful to avoid backseat driving (*conduite à l'arrière*).

# The Christ Moment
## Robert Beveridge

"I woke up and saw the lid of Sunday raise...it was the Christ
moment/that seemed before orgasm..."
—Clayton Eshleman, "Just Before Sunday Morning"

It grows
in dusty snow blown
in darkness, grey shine
when all electric lights
are out. The glow
from no one place,
anticipated fire ready
to ignite.
　　　　Clouds burn
away black linings;
perhaps, as horizon
turned again to sun,
it really was a face
above the clouds,
for just an instant.

# The Inexplicable Journey of the Taco Bell Lobster

Robert Beveridge

Your doctor says you're not
supposed to smoke the MAGA
apple, though you can get
the necessary equipment
to vaporize it at a handful
of new dispensaries around
the city. You ponder
how difficult it would be
to drop a few seeds, grow
your own on the down low,
maybe make a few extra bucks
from the locals with no scripts
and a whole bed full of Confederate
couture. There's a lot to be said
for complicity when all the colors
that matter are green, green,
green, and Granny Smith red.

# Hsi-wei and the Three Proverbs
## Robert Wexelblatt

The Tang minister Fang Xuan-ling devotes a lengthy section of his memoirs to the week-long visit he paid the peasant/poet Chen Hsi-wei. This was near the end of Hsi-wei's life, after the poet had given up his itinerant existence and settled in the tiny cottage granted him by the Governor of Chiangling. The place was in the middle of farmland three *li* outside the city gates, two rooms with a mean patio and a small vegetable garden.

Each day, Minister Fang would arrive from the city in the late morning and stay until sunset. He brought food, tea, wine, along with a scroll, an inkstone, and two brushes.

On the fourth afternoon, as they sat in the little patio taking tea, he asked about the poem Hsi-wei had titled "The Three Proverbs."

"Pardon my ignorance, Master, but the title is obscure to me. There are no proverbs in the poem. Perhaps you are aware that people call it 'Three Little Tales.'"

Hsi-wei grinned. "Titles are not so important to me. I was always pleased when people came up with their own names for my poor verses. I prefer them. All the same, choosing a title is a serious matter and seldom an easy one. Sometimes, a title was the real beginning of a poem; at others, a summary I added at the end. But most often, I thought of a title as a promise."

"A promise?"

"One that the poem attempts to fulfill. In rare cases, a title can be a key to unlock hidden meaning. The poem you've asked about is one of those."

"The poem is in code?"

"No, it's not a secret message. Just a silly puzzle."

"How so?"

"My Lord, an archer doesn't set up his target in order to

miss his aim, but I fear that is what happened with 'The Three Proverbs,' and you've confirmed it. The game was really for me more than the reader, which is where I went wrong. I was indulging myself. No doubt, people sensed this. Their title, 'Three Little Tales,' is better. 'Three Pointless Tales' would have been better still."

Fang leaned forward. "I'm not sure I understand. When you say you were indulging yourself and that poem is a puzzle, what do you mean?"

Hsi-wei refilled their teacups before replying.

"That unworthy little poem was an exercise I set myself. Two of the proverbs I heard as a child in my village; the third I picked up while traveling along the Grand Canal, which is where I wrote the poem."

"Ah," the attentive Fang said with satisfaction. "Then, each of the stories illustrates a proverb."

"Yes. And that was the puzzle for the reader, to figure out the proverbs. Unfortunately, the poem turned out to be like one of those ill-conceived jokes nobody gets. Or a lock without a key."

"But, the *title* was the key."

"As I said, a useless one. Actually, there's more to the matter. Behind each of the little made-up stories is a true one."

"So then, there are six stories and three proverbs?"

"Exactly. But now that you've gotten me thinking, I would like to say something about the difference between poems and proverbs. You could say that my relation to proverbs is one of a peasant, while my relation to poems is the consequence of my education in Daxing. So, the poem reflects my own ambiguous situation, too low-born ever to belong to the upper class, too educated to belong to the lower."

"Another way of looking at it is that your poems appeal to both classes. That is unusual, Master."

"You're most gracious to say so. If you're right, then perhaps that too is the consequence of my belonging to neither."

Here, Minister Fang drew out his scroll and prepared the ink.

"Please go on, Master. I would like to learn more of your views on poems and proverbs."

Hsi-wei was pleased to oblige.

"A poem is made by one person. It may be bad or good. If bad, it will be forgotten at once, maybe even by the one who made it. But if it is good, a poem may be remembered for a time. Some may memorize it and recite it at parties to divert or impress their guests. This is what passes for immortality among poets, who can be childishly vain. But a proverb comes from the people, even those sayings ascribed to Confucius or Lao-tse, because, by repeated application to their lives, the people make a proverb their own. Because a good proverb is owned by no one, it belongs to everyone."

Fang made a few notes, then returned to the matter that really interested him.

"What are the stories behind the stories in your poem?"

"Oh, it's been so long. Wendi was still Emperor when I made up that little puzzle."

Fang readied his brush and begged Hsi-wei to try to remember.

"Very well, I'll do my best for you. As you'll remember, this was during my journey along the Grand Canal, which has made so much money but cost more lives than all the Sui wars put together. Somewhere between Suzhou and Wuxi, I came to a town, set my sign up in the square as usual, and took orders for straw sandals. The town was busy; it had a depot, and many barges stopped there. A red-faced bargeman with a body like a crate ordered a pair of sandals from me. He growled that he would buy them on condition that I had them ready by the next morning when he would be moving on. He was curt and seemed inexplicably angry."

Hsi-wei paused. "Have you observed, my Lord, that people find it harder to conceal their anger than their sorrow?"

"Yes. That's quite true."

"In that respect, being angry is like knowing a humorous story. It wants to be told. Anyway, the bargeman said, 'I'd buy another pair for my wretched assistant, but the dog's-head can go barefoot. Let him get splinters!'

"I asked what the wretched assistant had done to merit the splinters.

"'The fool neglected the sweep and drove us square into the dock. I have to pay for the damage. He's barricaded himself in the cabin, the coward, or I'd have given him fifty lashes!'

"'With respect, sir,' I said, 'how old is he, this assistant?'

"'Fourteen. He's big for his age, though.'

"'And has he done anything of the kind before?'

"'Yes! Last week he nearly made us collide with one of the heavy timber barges. We'd have been sunk for sure.'

"'And what did you do?' I asked sympathetically.

"'What did I do? Gave him two lashings, didn't I, one with my tongue and one with the bamboo. Both good hidings, too, though it seems I was too lenient.'

"It was obvious why the boy was hiding. The bargeman could not control his temper. I ventured to ask him if he would listen to some advice.

"The astonished fellow looked me up and down. 'From a sandal-maker?'

"I stood up straighter. 'Yes,' I replied, 'from this worthless sandal-maker.'

"The bargeman scoffed but said, 'Well, out with it.'

"At a stall close by, a woman was selling sweets.

"'First,' I said, 'calm yourself. Walk around the square. Take twenty deep breaths. Then go to that woman over there and buy a paper of her sweets. When you get back to your barge, use them to coax the boy out of the cabin. Speak softly and promise him a really good meal—one with both pork and fish—if you make it to Jianxing without any more mishaps.'

"'What? Sweets? Pork?'

"'Yes, and fish, too,' I said."

Hsi-wei folded his hands and fell silent.

"What? That's all?" asked Fang lifting his brush.

"Yes. It was seeing how incensed that bargeman was and

picturing the terrified boy that made me think of the old proverb I heard as a child."

"What proverb?"

Hsi-wei smiled slyly. "Just now, my memory seems to be working, so I'll relate the second incident, which also concerns a bargeman. I heard the story from the drinkers in a tavern where I spent a sleepless summer night. I remember it well, a rambling, ramshackle place with gray boards and green slime, right on the docks. It was terribly hot because of the low ceiling and crush of canal men.

"The story was about a certain bargeman, of course. I can't recall his name; perhaps it was Chin. Well, this Chin was ambitious. He used the family savings to buy a barge and was doing well, but to be comfortably prosperous didn't satisfy him. He wanted a four-pillared villa. He wanted to be bowed to on the streets. He wanted others working for him. So, he took the easy path, said the men at the tavern. I had the impression that they all knew this path rather well.

"Chin made contacts among the disreputable and struck deals with them. He began transporting untaxed cargo to the capital, where the profits were greatest. His crooked colleagues assured him the magistrate would make no difficulties.

"Before long, Chin bought a second barge, then a third. He picked out a piece of high ground and ordered plans for his four-pillared villa.

"But then a new magistrate was appointed in Jining. He was from Qingzhou and incorruptible. After he was approached with the offer of the same bribe accepted by his predecessor, the magistrate proclaimed that a substantial reward would be paid for information about anyone transporting untaxed goods.

"Within the week, Chin was arrested and a day later was kneeling before the magistrate's bench. There were two informants. One was the man he hired to take charge of his third barge; the other was his younger brother. The first he had paid too little, the second was not only envious but vengeful.

Chin had bullied and tyrannized over him all his life, in addition to appropriating his share of the family savings.

"Chin was lashed fifty times, had to pay a heavy fine, and his three barges were confiscated."

"A familiar story," said Fang. "It shows the wisdom of the three-year term for magistrates and forbidding them to serve in their native province. But, Master, what's the proverb?"

Hsi-wei smiled. "Please be patient, My Lord. There's still one more story to tell. It isn't either pleasant or short. This one has nothing to do with the canal or bargemen, but it does have another honest magistrate. His name was Guo Hui-liang, and I came to know him a little when I was studying with Shen Kuo in the capital. He had just passed his examination. Guo Hui-liang impressed me. He was learned and humane, a good Confucian intrigued by Buddhist teachings. Though he was from a well-off family, he showed sincere concern for the poor. Perhaps that is why he wished to meet me, the peasant who turned down a fortune for an education. As you know, I was then a curiosity, something like a trained dog. Guo and I met twice, and I enjoyed our conversations. A more upright and thoughtful man I did not come across in Daxing. That I turned up at his new post was a sheer accident.

"Magistrate Guo arrived in Yangchuan two months before I did. This was at the time of Emperor Wen's land reform, the Equal Field system. By the way, I'm pleased that Emperor Gaozu has decided to confirm it, a good and wise decision. According to Wendi's revolutionary system, the government became sole owner of all land in the Empire so that it could allocate it to individuals regardless of class. Land was distributed based on each household's ability to supply labor. The system transformed the situation of the poor but was not entirely fair or without problems. For example, the lands of high officials were exempted from tax and were inherited by their families at their deaths. Taxes for all other households were the same, so the burden fell heavily on peasants and not at all on officials. Normally, when the householder died, the land reverted to the state. This was to keep the local gentry from accumulating land and the power that went with it. But there was a hole in the law's fabric. Land could be passed down within the family if it required long-term development.

"Guo's predecessor in the district did nothing to implement the reforms. The wealthy of Yangchuan still controlled all the good land, and the lot of the peasants was to be their share-croppers, serfs, and servants.

"Guo arrived in Yangchuan with his four constables and escorted by only six cavalrymen. With such a small force, no one expected him to change things. But they were wrong. The day after his arrival, he ordered notices to be posted and sent his constables to summon the population to a public meeting. Three days later, Guo stood on a platform set up in the square dressed in his formal robes and wearing his winged hat. He explained to a large crowd that the new system meant all land in the district would now be reallocated by him as soon as a census was taken of men, women, and livestock. Each household, he promised, would be counted and issued its land fairly, according to the new law. I was told that the peasants set up a loud cheer after he finished speaking. The well-off were silent.

"The rich did all they could to thwart Guo. They offered bribes to the census-takers, tried to intimidate the constables, and threatened their share-croppers and serfs. The most cunning of them even tried to use the law to defeat the law."

Minister Fang, who had ceased taking notes and seemed to be losing interest, perked up at that last phrase and asked, "How did he do that?"

"You remember the exception for long-term development?"

"We've retained that provision. It's sensible to let one family hold on to their land if they are carrying out projects like swamp-clearing, the cultivation of orchards, and digging irrigation systems. Those can take years."

"Exactly. This rascally landowner instructed his friends to import eight mulberry trees each and plant two in each corner of their land. They all filed petitions claiming they were establishing a local silk industry."

"I see. How did the magistrate react?"

"He found out which of the census-takers had taken bribes and punished them publicly. He reassured the frightened peasants that he would protect them. As for the mulberry plantings, he dismissed all the petitions, pointing out that they had planted red mulberries and silkworms ate the fruit of white mulberries, also that neither the worms nor the saplings would be likely to survive Yangchuan's severe winters."

"Good for him, knowing about the red mulberries."

"The nobles didn't give up. Instead, they slandered Guo, spreading rumors that he was guilty of three outrages. First, that he had seduced the third wife of a rich landowner. Second, that he had misappropriated government funds. Third, that he had sent his constables to burn down one of their villas. Through their connections in the capital, they managed to get these false charges into the hands of the First Minister."

"Had they any proof?"

"The third wife was bullied by her husband into signing a false affidavit. A villa really did burn down, but because of a cook's carelessness. As for the misappropriated funds, they claimed that Guo had bought himself a dozen silk robes and a pair of prime horses. As evidence, they submitted forged receipts."

"What happened?"

"I arrived in time to witness the outcome. I heard the truth from Guo himself when I paid a call on him the day before the provincial prefect arrived to conduct a hearing. I attended it, of course. One rich landowner after another repeated their lies. The disgraced third wife was cross-examined but said almost nothing before breaking down in sobs."

"Was Guo able to defend himself?"

Hsi-wei shrugged. "He did what he could."

"Didn't anyone speak up for him?"

"Only one person."

"Not his constables?"

"No. One was beaten half to death, and the others were offered the choice of the same treatment or a bribe."

"None of the peasants spoke for him?"

"None said a word. Some were clearly frightened; others may have believed the rumors, but many seemed pleased to see a magistrate in the dock, even a good one. The hearing ended with the prefect ordering Guo to return to the capital under guard. As the crowd was drifting away, I overheard one peasant say to another, 'It's just as well. It's dangerous to have a magistrate who can't be bribed.'"

"Who was the one who spoke up for Guo?"

Hsi-wei glumly looked down at his lap.

"Only this worthless maker of straw-sandals and useless poems."

After that, the two men sat quietly for a while, watching the sun set. Fang was shocked by what that peasant had said about upright officials. Then he spread out his scroll and took up his brush.

"So, Master Hsi-wei, I understand these are the stories behind the three in your poem. But what are the proverbs?"

Hsi-wei counted them out on his fingers.

"Strike with a meat bun. Water floats a boat but also sinks it. Virtue is more persecuted by the wicked than loved by the good."

## THE THREE PROVERBS

*Fu discovered Dao chewing a pair of his breeches.*
*He bawled at the dog and beat him with a stick.*
*Dao hid himself behind the pig shed all afternoon.*
*Just before supper, Dao dragged off a sandal.*
*Fu swore at the dog and threw a brass ladle at him.*
*Fu's old mother watched from the hearth.*
*She held a meat bun out toward the cowering Dao*
*then called him close and quietly stroked his head.*

*Dreaming of fishing, trade, warm starry nights*
*on the canal, Dingxiao and his son decided to build*
*a sampan, one with comfortable quarters for two.*
*They laid the first plank flat, affixed two for the sides,*
*smoothed and sealed it all with tar. Two weeks hard work.*
*"Let's launch!" begged the son. Dingxiao tied the prow to a willow.*
*The hull floated. Proud and weary, they slept through the*
*cloudburst. Come morning, only the rope was above water.*

*Bingwen was diligent, the smartest, best behaved.*
*Master Shu praised him relentlessly. "Admire Bingwen's*
*calligraphy! See how neatly he keeps his brushes!*
*Hear how perfectly he recites the Shijing Masters!"*
*Every day the other boys found new ways*
*to torment Bingwen. They tore off his cap,*
*pummeled his ribs, tripped him up, and the angriest*
*cursed his ancestors to the eighteenth generation.*

# A Long Walk Through Time
Catherine Dowling

Outside the enormous window of the hotel restaurant, rain pours down in dense, monsoon-like sheets that have been falling since before dawn. We're surrounded by mountains, but I can see them only as hulking shadows behind the enveloping grayness. I nibble at pastries, try the muesli. Around 10 am, the downpour becomes a drizzle, and the monochrome terrain takes on a faint green tinge. I know if I wait long enough, the veil of gray will lift to reveal a panorama of mountain and valley; what I don't know is that it will also reveal a story that reaches across three centuries and two continents.

So, I wait and watch. An hour later, when the sun bursts through the blanket of cloud, I'm rewarded for my vigilance; the land is transformed into a panoply of every shade of green imaginable, dazzling and intense it seems surreal. I grab my camera and my umbrella and head out of the hotel.

I'm at a conference in Delphi, County Mayo, on the west coast of Ireland. I'm from Ireland, but I've grown so used to the red and ochre vastness of New Mexico where I live that the closeness of the mountains feels momentarily claustrophobic. Cushiony green, they draw you upwards. There's a promise of mystery, an alluring hint of wildness waiting at the top. But I take an educated guess that all that greenery floats on a bed of waterlogged turf. If you don't know which tufts of grass to step on, you can be sucked knee-deep into the murky brown bog. I leave the mountains to the sheep.

Delphi is at the southern end of the glacial Doolough Valley. The only way into or out of the place is the tiny, two-lane R335 road snaking past the hotel on its way north to Clew Bay, where John Lennon once owned an island. The surrounding villages and townlands have names like Thullabaun, Cloonamanagh,

Killadoon, Derryheigh, words that lilt and sing and sometimes twist the tongue, which is why the name Delphi stands out. My hotel, the Delphi Resort, seems isolated, but I know around a few bends of the R335 lies Delphi Lodge, a more old-money affair that I want to visit before it starts to rain again.

I follow the road north to an old bridge that crosses the Bundorragha River. A man looks over the stone wall into the river; presumably, the owner of the small van parked close enough to the road to get clipped by passing traffic, if there were any passing traffic.

"The salmon are running," he says without looking at me.

He's right. Spawning fish glint just beneath the surface, racing instinctively towards their past. The Oscar-winning movie, The Quiet Man was filmed in these parts in 1951. One of the most famous scenes takes place on a bridge like this one; a brooding John Wayne hears the voice of his dead mother leading him back to his ancestral homestead and into the arms of tempestuous Maureen O'Hara. I glance at the man to my left. Not as tall as John Wayne, certainly, but then I'm no Maureen O'Hara.

"I must come back with me rod," he grunts, eyes down, and heads for the van.

Oh well, the movie was silly anyway. I move on.

A small lake, Fin Lough, is visible over the wild red fuchsia that lines the roadside. On the far side, a couple of small, white fishing boats bob gently against the backdrop of a sheer emerald slope. I stop, arrested by the intensity of the color, the reward for enduring all that rain. Delphi Lodge, my destination, lies just ahead at the end of a curving, tree-lined drive, its grounds open to walkers. The building's elegant floor-to-ceiling windows reflect a panorama of lake and valley and the ever-changing weather. I pause to read the brochure I picked up somewhere, probably in Dublin.

The lodge, now a hotel, was built in the early 19th century as a sporting retreat for Lord Altamont, the 2nd Marquess of Sligo, an often-absentee lord who spent much of the year in

London. The Delphi estate stretches to over 1,000 acres—in Ireland, a substantial amount of land. The Greek god, Zeus, decreed Delphi on the southern slopes of Mount Parnassus to be the center of the world. Lord Altamont, I read, is the one who, Zeus-like, named his lodge after the center of the world because he thought the Doolough Valley resembled Delphi in Greece. The house I'm looking at is not the original Lodge, but its elegant lines and symmetrical proportions are beautiful.

A man walks ahead of me. He's elderly, in his 80s perhaps, but solidly built. He wears a dark wool suit, the kind that lasts forever, the kind you can't get anymore. The jacket is shiny in spots and creased with the bending and straightening of his body over the years. I remember as a child, every old farmer seemed to live in a suit like that. His black and white Collie walks at his side, a hint of stiffness in her gait. In dog years, they're probably the same age.

"*Breá, bog,*" he mutters as I pass him. I wonder if all the men in these parts are parsimonious with words. I'm surprised at the language, though; this isn't a *Gaeltacht*, an Irish-speaking area. But his two words are spot on. Now that the sun has come out, it is a *fine* summer day, and the air is soft on the skin.

I want to reply, but my grasp of Irish is so weak that I can't remember the correct response. "How old is your dog?" I ask instead, in English.

The dog is eleven. Not quite as old as her master, but they're both sprightly for their age. I tell him I'm staying in the hotel down the road. He tells me they're from *an tuaisceart*, the north, which could mean anywhere, taking a stroll "to stretch the animal's legs." We walk the path together past the lake, into the trees. The ground is spongy and pungent from rain, an earthy, wholesome smell of things dying and things growing. I try to fill in the silences that my companion seems perfectly comfortable with, but I struggle to form complete sentences in Irish. He picks up on the trace of American in my accent and asks where I'm living.

"Indian country," he pronounces when I tell him

Albuquerque. It makes a change from the "Is it really like Breaking Bad?" that I usually get.

Inspired perhaps by our proximity to the ghost of John Wayne, I jump to the myopic conclusion that the only way he could know about the Native American population of New Mexico—there are 19 native pueblos in the state—is through cowboy movies. "You like westerns?" I ask.

"I read," he says so casually that for a moment, I'm not sure he said anything at all. It's the rebuke I deserve. I reach down to pet the dog, embarrassed, while the silence stretches ahead of us.

"They come here, you know," he says as we round a slight bend. I've no idea what he's talking about.

"Indians! They come here. The Famine Walk," he inclines his head towards the Lodge, now hidden behind a wall of leaves that moves in the breeze. I sense some exasperation with my ignorance. "They walked from Louisburgh to here during the famine. The Indians come for the commemorations. The Choctaw."

Now he's beginning to make sense. The Great Hunger, an *Gorta Mór*, began in 1845 when the potato crop failed. A mold called *Phytophthora infestans*, seen first in New York in 1843, caused the tubers to rot in the ground before they could be harvested. Accounts from the era talk about the stench emanating from the potato fields and emaciated typhus-ridden corpses lying by roadsides. Frederick Douglass, the American abolitionist and former slave, toured Ireland in 1845, promoting his autobiography, and was shocked by the poverty he witnessed. By the time the famine ended in 1850, nearly a million people had died from starvation or disease. There were many forced Famine Walks. People walked to find food at soup kitchens; they walked to find employment in one of the "workhouses" managed by the local Poor Law Union or walked to ports in Dublin or Cork where they boarded ships for New York or Grosse-Île in Canada.

But where do the Choctaw from Oklahoma fit in?

"They gave us money," he says. I wait for more, but nothing comes.

At another bend in the path, he calls the dog and turns back in the direction from which we came. "She gets sore from walking," he explains, then adds, "They have computers in that hotel of yours. Look it up." He raises his hand slightly as he walks away, "*Slán.*"

"*Slán leath*," I say to his back, remembering how to say goodbye.

I continue walking until the clouds thicken overhead. As I speed past Fin Lough on the way back to the hotel, the green and blue of land and lake retreat once more into gray. I make it back before the rain starts and open my laptop.

I've studied the famine—what Irish person hasn't?—but to me, as an undergraduate, it was a tragedy that belonged to another century, part of the history of the British occupation that my generation was decisively moving on from. Yet, these new dimensions— Delphi Lodge, Native Americans—intrigue me. They certainly didn't appear in my college texts. When I type "famine walk Mayo" into the search engine, Google is more forthcoming.

In the 1790s, before building the lodge, Lord Altamont ordered the construction of a village about 12 miles north of Delphi. He named it Louisburgh after a town in Nova Scotia. The potato blight hit many places in Europe, including Britain. Only in Ireland did it cause wide-scale famine. Throughout the famine, boatloads of food left Ireland for England and far-flung parts of the British Empire, food sold to pay rent to landlords like Lord Altamont, food the British government refused to stop exporting. The peasants who worked the land were forced to rely almost exclusively on the potato. Mayo was one of the most potato-dependent counties in the country. By 1849, the well-designed little village of Lousiburgh and the surrounding area had been decimated by four years of famine.

On March 30, 1849, Colonel Hogrove and Captain Primrose from the Poor Law Union passed through

Louisburgh. The Poor Law Union administered welfare to the poor. Hogrove and Primrose were supposed to assess the eligibility of the peasantry to receive a few pounds of grain. They told the people of the area to report to them in Delphi Lodge early on the 31st for the assessment.

Estimates vary, but as many as 600 people, adults, and children walked overnight from Lousiburgh to Delphi. The smoothly paved N335 didn't exist in 1849, so the hungry, often barefoot peasants trudged through sleety, mist-shrouded Doolough Pass. The next day, they were sent away from the Lodge empty-handed. Estimates of the number of people who died on the walk vary, but it was likely in the hundreds. The first Mayo Famine Walk commemorating the tragedy was organized in 1988 and has taken place every May ever since. But what of the Choctaw?

The Smithsonian Magazine online explains the connection. Fifteen years before the Irish famine began, over 4,000 miles away in Mississippi, the Choctaw tribes that my taciturn companion mentioned signed the Treaty of Dancing Rabbit Creek, ceding the last of their tribal lands to the United States. Between 1831 and 1833, over 20,000 Choctaw walked the 500-mile Trail of Tears to new land in Oklahoma. Thousands died on the way, more perished while struggling to set up homes in the new Indian Territory. Yet in 1847, Choctaw elders somehow got word that people were starving to death in Ireland. In the midst of their own desperate poverty, they collected $710 to send to Ireland for famine relief.

I watch a YouTube video of Chief Hollis Roberts of the Choctaw Nation as he hiked past Doo Lough in 1990. The day is bright and blustery, and as he walks, Roberts is interviewed about his own people's Trail of Tears. I am so moved by the Choctaw Nation's generosity that I decide to forego the last day of the conference and walk some of the trail myself.

I start the morning with the hotel's more than adequate breakfast, pack snacks, and a bottle of water on top of the rain gear in my backpack. Not exactly an authentic 1849 experience.

I briefly consider leaving the pack behind but think better of it.

The day is bright and warm, in the high 70s, perfect for walking. I cross the bridge again—no salmon today—and take the road past the Lodge. Rhododendrons, fat and waxy, crowd together on the ditches with fuchsia, grass, and an intense green moss. Plants are abundant here. Wild ferns uncurl beneath the canopy of trees, and something green seems to burst from every inch of ground. But as I move north, past stone cottages and tiny marked-off fields, the vegetation thins out. By the time I catch sight of Doo Lough, the land is bare of trees and fields, just grass, bog cotton, and tufts of heather sweeping up the mountains on both sides of the lake.

The Doo in Doo Lough comes from the Irish *dubh*, meaning black. Clouds move across the sky, and where they block the sun, the lake does appear inky black and uninviting. But when the clouds pass, the water turns dark blue, rippling and sparkling in the sunshine. The land here is untamed, and through gaps in the mountains, I catch glimpses of other empty valleys and imagine other isolated mountain lakes.

It's a lonely place, but in the clear morning light, I find it uplifting—and difficult to imagine what it was like on that frigid night in March 1849. So, I decide to endure a little hardship. I take off my hiking boots and socks. The road is cool and a little rough, but my foot comes down on some pebbles every so often. The pain they cause is out of proportion to their size. I stop to dip my feet in a little stream that rushes down from the mountains sinking beneath the road on its way to the lake. The water is cold but soothing. I decide to end the half-hearted experiment in hardship, put my shoes back on and keep walking.

The day is so beautiful, the land so absorbing, that I almost miss the famine memorial just north of the lake. It's slightly elevated on what looks like limestone with a small parking space in front of it. The monument is a large piece of gray stone carved into the shape of a crucifix. It resembles the Celtic stone crosses that can be found all over Ireland, but where they are decorated with intricate, interlaced patterns, this cross is crude and unadorned. It seems appropriate. The inscriptions on the base, however, are not what I expect.

The plaque on the north side of the memorial tells me it was erected by AFrI, Action From Ireland, an organization that works to influence social justice and human rights policy in Ireland and abroad, and was unveiled in 1994 by Karen Gearon. That's a name I remember. She was a shop steward in Dunnes Stores, one of Ireland's biggest supermarket chains. In 1984, in protest against apartheid, she and ten colleagues refused to handle South African produce. Their strike lasted nearly three years, transforming public opinion until the Irish government finally banned the importation of produce from South Africa.

The inscription on the southern side reads, "In 1991 we walked AFrI's Great Famine Walk at Doolough. And soon afterward we walked the road to freedom in South Africa," a quote from Archbishop Desmond Tutu. The front plaque says, "To commemorate the hungry poor who walked here in 1849 and walk the third world today. Freedom for South Africa." It's followed by a quote from Gandhi, "How can men feel honored by the humiliation of their fellow beings?"

I sit on the rocks and pull out of my pack the pages I printed late last night. I read about all the people who have walked this road: members of the Choctaw Nation, Desmond Tutu, Vedran Smailovic, the Cellist of Sarajevo, the children of Chernobyl, Kim Phúc, the little girl running naked and burned by napalm in the haunting Vietnam War photograph. This, I realize, is more than a commemoration of an Irish tragedy; it's a point of connection for people from all over the world who suffer injustice.

By the time he left Ireland, Frederick Douglass believed the cause of the slave in the United States was the cause of the oppressed everywhere. But it seems to me now that the connection between people Douglass identified doesn't just transcend nationality; it transcends time. Remembering a tragedy that happened nearly 200 years ago has agency in the present. The Dunnes Stores strikers have helped promote equality in South Africa. Irish people have walked the Trail of Tears to raise money for famine relief in Somalia; Mary Robinson, Ireland's first female president, is an honorary Choctaw chief. In gratitude for their generosity, the Irish government funds a scholarship for Choctaw youth to study in Ireland. My "get over it, move on" attitude to history is, I think, untenable.

Clouds begin to mass overhead, turning the lake black. If I hurry, I might be able to beat the rain. I put the pages away, take a quick drink of water, and begin my long walk back to Delphi.

# Passing By
## George Moore

*Ventspils, Latvia*

Early morning and the forest path is empty
but for the woman sweeping with a broom of sticks

moving leaves off the packed dirt with twigs cut
of black wood. And the city may not see her

like the last worker doing her chore on a Soviet morning
dusting the dust from the trail gathering leaves

into dark shadows. She sweeps in long curves
in a kind of dance solitary and intent on her partner

the anima in a veil of trees. Like clockwork each day
in my self-absorbed run I come upon her.

She does not look up nor move more than a foot
to either side. But the path is her line through history

the forest her country loosed from the grip of commissars
and she sweeps with a sense of freedom.

If I or the city do not see her it does not matter.
She cleans where once she moved dirt and leaves.

# Isle of Mull
## George Moore

A mull seems but a half-built hill and older
still than mountains I've known

round and bald as my father's head
which I've tried so many times to climb

before he was gone and the mulls
remain princely but unglorified

I park on the roadside where a hint of trail
ascends up through the grass humps and stone

thinking if I am here I should really have
a trophy for my time a climb a peak

and so I climb into the late morning fog
till shale becomes a four-point scramble

slick as the devil's tongue
hand over hand on a grassy vertical

and the top a noll a rounded bump
a field from which my father's bald head shines

where the isle rolls out on a gentle wind
and standing where a great great grandfather

may have stood before we both descend
careful too as tourists have died by a false step

and then down to the car
and the inn and a cup of tea

and a sort of unconscious bereavement
as I've been thinking of the dead all day

with the calm brewed in single clouds
above a few slow sculpted sheep

grazing undisturbed on
the new sprouts of their hillsides

# We, the Melungeons
James Gallant

Susan Taylor, her flight on hold, seated herself on a bench at Atlanta International Airport. Hundreds of people also grounded were milling about.

"Never knowed a plane couldn't lift off in hot weather," said the white-haired man in a jeans-suit seated down the bench a way.

Susan smiled restrainedly.

"Temperature's a hundred and five out there, they say. I stepped outside a while ago, sweated like a whore in church. My name's Harold. I'm going to visit my son in Pittsburgh."

Harold's stab at familiarity reminded her of similar efforts at the thirtieth reunion of her 1967 high school class in Bristol, Tennessee, earlier that week.

She rose from her seat and resumed walking.

Following the reunion, she'd rented a car and driven down to Atlanta for a second nostalgic get-together—with her college roomie Tina Lockwood. About all Tina and she had in common these days were reminiscences of college days, and those were pretty well exhausted the evening Susan arrived. Should old acquaintance be forgot and never brought to mind? She wasn't sure there was an alternative.

Waiting to have her hair done in Syracuse before leaving for the South, she'd happened on a magazine article about the American passion for reunions that generated "together atmospheres." For people related technically in some way, but separated as Americans commonly were by mobility, economic status, education—or whatever—reunions stirred social instincts at once magnetic and likely to disappoint.

Supposedly every cell in the human body was replaced by others in the course of a decade. Her class reunion made that easy to believe. After thirty years, altered faces, voices, and figures had rendered many of her classmates unrecognizable. The Elvis-resembling quarterback of the football team was palsied; the nubile blond homecoming queen looked like a lineman; the ugly duckling teenage girl had become a middle-aged swan. There had been intimations of psychological transformations as radical as the physical, but to explore those at a two-day gathering resembling an extended cocktail party would have been impossible.

Susan felt she'd had enough "together atmosphere" to last a lifetime.

News spread at the airport that the hazard of hot, dry air preventing airliner takeoffs was about to be replaced by another: a storm with tornadic potential bearing down on the region. She was likely to be marooned at the airport indefinitely.

She paid four dollars for a bag of corn chips and three for a bottle of water, and her thoughts turned to entertainment. She regretted having left books in her now-inaccessible luggage.

She was in a Southern-flavored gift-and-book shop perusing titles when one caught her eye: *The Melungeons Reconsidered.* "Melungeon" was a term out of her Tennessee youth, a synonym for "boogeyman." ("If you don't behave," mothers would say to their kids, "the Melungeons gonna get you!") The thrust of this admonition had been clear enough, although it wasn't until Susan was in high school that she discovered Melungeons were a reclusive dark-skinned people residing up in the Appalachian Mountains not far from her hometown Bristol. An English teacher had assigned a folktale purporting to explain Melungeon origins: Satan, weary of his shrewish wife, abandoned Hell and went abroad looking for new digs. Arrived in the high-ridge Appalachians where nothing much grew but briars and scrub trees, he felt right at home. He settled there, took an Indian wife, and produced a large brood of dark, devilish offspring given to looting, killing, and burning—the original Melungeons.

Susan started at the author's name on the book cover, Tom

Collins. She flipped to the back flyleaf for the author's headshot and bio. Never mind the receding hairline and horn-rimmed glasses, this was undoubtedly *the* Tom Collins one year ahead of her in high school in Bristol, her first boyfriend. According to the bio, he was now a professor of folklore at Georgia State University in Atlanta.

She purchased the book, published recently by a Southern academic press, and found a seat with decent light to begin reading. *The Melungeons Reconsidered* was an overview of research on these dusky mountain people that had been inspired by Kingsport, Tennessee, native Brent Kennedy's 1994 *The Melungeons: The Resurrection of a Proud People.* Questions about Kennedy's own ancestry had inspired his interest in the Melungeons. His elders had led him to believe his ancestry was Celtic, "black Irish," and his straight black hair and blue eyes might have testified to such origins. But the black Irish had milk-white skin. *His* was tawny, and why did his brother look like Saddam Hussein?

Susan looked up from the page. She had an uncle who looked Middle Eastern.

Kennedy had discovered that his physical traits resembled closely those of many Appalachian Melungeons and Louisiana Creoles who had sub-Saharan African and Indian elements in their DNA. He knew that his American ancestors had moved about with inexplicable frequency in the mountainous regions of Western Virginia and Eastern Kentucky, and there were vague stories about land they'd owned being confiscated. Melungeons in the nineteenth century were not permitted to own property.

Kennedy's speculations about his racial background had interested Tom Collins, who had similar physical characteristics. He, too, had been led to believe his heritage was Scotch-Irish.

Susan shared the two authors' black hair, light brown skin, and blue eyes, and she, too, had been led to believe her origins were in the British Isles. Tom's list of common Melungeon surnames included not only Collins but *Gibson*—her maiden name.

She was in Atlanta. Tom, who taught there, presumably lived there. She reached into her purse for her cellphone and, in a few minutes, was talking to Tom in his office at Georgia State, describing her situation at the airport, the discovery of his book, and the curiosity it aroused concerning her own ancestry. "Do you remember how when we dated in high school, we were told we looked like kin?"

"I remembered it as I was doing my research," Tom said, "and we *could* be distant cousins if both of us had Melungeon ancestors. Those families in the mountains intermarried a lot."

"You think your ancestry was Melungeon?"

"I do increasingly, although my family's genealogy is obscure."

"Mine, too."

"Melungeons who escaped into civilization would have wanted to forget their past because they had a reputation for being tricky, if not out-and-out criminal. They were as distrusted as black people, and of course, many of them *had* black blood and looked the part. They were outcasts, non-persons. They couldn't own property and had no legal rights."

"How would they have managed to escape the mountains?"

"Not all Melungeons looked the part."

"Your ancestors and mine didn't."

"That would be a good guess...The weather has you trapped at the airport, you say?"

"Forever, I think."

"When you called, I was just about to leave my office. It would be great to see you again. I could be down there in a half-hour."

"That would be wonderful," Susan said, although her recent experience of old acquaintance suggested it might *not* be.

———■ ✦ ■———

Tom managed to locate her in the crowd. There were smiles of recognition, quick appraisals of each other's physical appearance, a light embrace. He was chunkier than the last time they embraced.

Tom waved an inclusive hand over the mass of people shuffling about aimlessly or gazing up slack-jawed at television screens. "They should post that sign Dante had at the gate of Hell: 'Abandon hope, all ye who enter here.'"

"They have little rooms with beds you can rent," Susan said. "You can nap for forty-two dollars an hour."

Tom shook his head.

They found seats together.

"Your commenting on my book is stranger than you may imagine," Tom said. "Starting tomorrow, there's to be a first-ever gathering of Melungeons up at Clinch Valley College up in Wise, Virginia."

The public address voice interrupted Tom with further information about flight delays.

Susan groaned.

"Does that include you?"

Susan nodded. "I'll still be here at midnight."

"You seem as interested in this Melungeon business as I am."

"I am."

"How important is it that you get back to Syracuse right away?"

"Not very."

"As I was driving down here, I had an idea. I'm driving up to Wise tomorrow. Would you want to come along? Jenny and I could put you up here tonight."

It would be an adventure, and after her disappointing reunions, she was in the mood for one.

———— ✦ ————

As Tom and she drove north on the freeway toward Atlanta, Susan inquired about the origin of the term 'Melungeon.'

"No one really knows," Tom said. "It may have come from the French *mélange*—mixtures."

"Racial mixtures?"

Tom nodded. "Melungeons are racially complex. There's likely to be Indian and African blood in them. You can often tell that just by looking at them. Kennedy thinks Turks got into the mix, and Turks *were* mongrels long before they got here."

"*Turks?*"

"The Portuguese and Spanish in America early on had Turkish slaves. Kennedy has described words in American Indian languages with parallels in Turkish or Arabic. He thinks Turkish slaves may have been the original settlers in the mountains, not the Scotch-Irish."

"Why is the Melungeon gathering at Wise?"

"It's near the borders of Virginia, Tennessee, and Kentucky—Melungeon central. Clinch Valley College there has offered its dormitories and cafeterias."

"What will it be like?"

"Don't ask me. There's never been one before."

Susan sat at the kitchen island of Tom's spacious Virginia Highlands bungalow, getting acquainted with Tom's wife Jenny, a slender, tallish, pretty woman with Asian features. She busied about the kitchen, preparing a meal for the three of them.

"Tom and you certainly *look* as if you came from the same stock," Jenny observed, "but neither of you look like the Melungeons in Tom's book. *They* look like either African-Americans or Indians."

"When there's white blood in the mix, Melungeons don't necessarily look the part," Tom observed.

"Tom and I were both told back home that we were black Irish," Susan said.

"Our parents and grandparents may have been liars— or people who had been lied to," Tom put in, "because Melungeons were regarded as disreputable outcasts."

"But how did some manage to *become* reputable?" Susan asked.

"Well, if you claimed to be Irish or Jewish or Spanish and looked the part, you might pass muster. How you were classified depended largely on appearance."

"You two could pass for Spanish," Jenny observed.

"What are *your* origins," Susan asked Jenny.

"I'm a Polipeno."

Susan grinned. "A *what*?"

"Polish father, Filipino mother. My parents met in the Philippines during the Second World War."

"By the way, Susan," Tom put in, "some recent DNA studies have suggested that Scots and Irish may have at least as much in common genetically with the Basques in northwestern Spain as with Celts. There's also some evidence that peoples from the Mediterranean may have migrated to the British Isles long before the Celts arrived in 2500 BC."

"My head's spinning," Susan said.

"There are Melungeons who will tell you tell a story about a mutiny aboard a Portuguese ship that was sailing the Atlantic coast. The sailors strung up the captain and burned the ship. Then they made their way into the mountains. They might have had black or Indian wives there. But the Portuguese were a racial mix already. They had colonies in southwestern Africa."

Jenny's obligations in Atlanta prevented her from accompanying Tom and Susan to Wise. "Good thing, too," she said. "If I turned up at Wise with my slant eyes, things would *really* get messy."

"I've reserved a room for myself in one of the Clinch dorms," Tom said. "When we get to Wise, we'll get one for you, Susan."

Many miles north of Atlanta, they were still passing recently built strip malls, schools, apartment complexes, suburban "ranchers," and split-level houses—accommodations for the swelling population of the region. Interspersed amid the novelties were abandoned driftwood-gray farmhouses and outbuildings. At a major intersection, opposite a fast-food restaurant in hot red and yellow colors, gray vertical tombstones leaned at angles to the perpendicular amid the weedy growth of a forgotten rural cemetery. A rusty gate hung precariously from one rusty hinge.

A farmer was storing hay in an abandoned one-room red brick schoolhouse with a modest bell tower. Hay bulged from raw window openings.

The terrain rose steadily from the Georgia piedmont. Ninety miles north of Atlanta, they were in the Blue Ridge Mountains, and there were mountains around them the rest of the way to Wise, where a crowd swarmed the parking lots of the Clinch Valley College dormitories.

Tom reached Brent Kennedy by phone and discovered that over six hundred people had registered for the gathering, a surprisingly large number. Finding a room for Susan on campus would be impossible. Tom arranged for her to stay at the Holiday Inn five miles down the road in Norton.

That evening, they sat in the grass on the Clinch State College campus in a crowd eating hot dogs, beans, and potato salad. There were tawny Mediterranean and coal-black African skins, high Indian cheekbones, archaic feather headdresses, Middle Eastern fezzes, Jewish noses. A middle-aged man near where Tom and Susan were sitting looked a *lot* like Saddam Hussein.

Snippets of conversations overheard:

"*Your* family buried food to keep it cold? Jeez, I thought we was the only ones did that!"

"My husband's folks claimed they descended from survivors of the Indian raid on the Roanoke Island colony."

"*We* were told we came from the Lost Tribe of Israel. But my sister thought our forefathers were probably Gypsies."

"Yeah, the lost tribe of *India*."

Laughter.

"Mumma said she was always scrubbing her face when she was a little girl, tryin' to make it come white. Her Daddy said, 'Honey, you may as well stop. I been trying to do that my whole life, it don't work.'"

"We'd come down out of the mountains when I was a kid. Didn't do it very often, 'cause they stared at us funny."

"My great-aunt Mabel said we were Sioux Indians back when. The last name on Dad's side was originally 'Duck.'"

"Was there a Donald Duck?"

"They changed it finally from 'Duck' to 'Hall.' But one of them insisted on calling himself Samuel Adams."

"After the beer?"

"Brent Kennedy thinks a lot of us were Turks."

"Yeah, we were Turks. At the first Thanksgiving, we had Shish Kebab."

"The mayor of Wise flew to Turkey awhile back, let the Turks know we came from there."

"I'll bet the Turks were excited to hear that."

"The mayor of some Turkey town sent a message back with the guy from here. Said it was nice that we got back in touch."

"I thought Turkey Town was in Alabama?"

———■ ✦ ■———

The scene of the First Union banquet, the next afternoon, was the conference room at the Holiday Inn in Norton where Susan was staying.

Television cameras and reporters crowded the hallway outside the banquet room, and there were vendors hawking FIRST UNION t-shirts and "Melungeon and Proud" buttons.

A cinnamon-skinned vendor with straight black hair whose nametag identified him as "M. Mehmet Topeck" sat at a card table beneath a sign, EXPLORE YOUR TURKISH ORIGINS, handing out postcards adorned with colorful Turkish scenes advertising upcoming tours of Anatolia.

Following the banquet meal served buffet-style, the mayor of Wise, who'd gone to Turkey, described a documentary film in production at Istanbul by an American crew, to be titled "The Melungeons: a Forgotten People."

Historian Eloy Gallegos spoke of his recent research concerning soldiers from northern Spain who'd constructed forts in Georgia, North Carolina, and Tennessee early on.

Brent Kennedy remarked in his keynote address that what had become abundantly clear, amid all the uncertainty about the Melungeons' origins, was that the conventional all-white version of the first settlement of the Appalachians was fiction. The original Americans there had very likely been Spanish, Portuguese, African, and Turkish, in addition to Native American.

"The truth the Melungeon story tells is that we Americans, whatever our origins, are New World brothers and sisters. Racial prejudice and injustice can have no place here. We may never know for sure what our racial background may have been, and if it's proven eventually that we have no genetic relation to the Turks, the Portuguese, or whomever—so what? Let's all just pretend we're related and see what happens!"

Susan reflected that to have discovered her ancestry might be Melungeon (whatever *that* might mean) was interesting but seemed about as fragile a basis for brotherhood and sisterhood as graduating from the same public high school the same year. She'd thought after leaving Tina Lockwood's house in Atlanta that she'd had enough "together atmosphere" to last a lifetime, but here she was immersed in a dense cloud of it, American as apple pie.

# Far Beyond, Years Later
DAH

I saw the seasons in you
there in the tracks of moon
this is how I remember:

from girl
  to woman

        lover

Like a journey of layers
the seasons weaved baskets
where blind love tossed words

I felt all that I could feel
your impassive eyes
like two dark birds

Far beyond, years later
this emptiness, a hole
set in place

appearing then disappearing
like a watermark
stamped on memory

# Isabella
## DAH

A small hand of rain opens
kicking up the dust that hangs
like fables from books

The sun, a broken candlemaker
tucked into the horizon
A breeze taunts the cracked leaves

Between us love was tribal
the conjuring of eyes
the tinder, kindling, flames

and your body, an ebony vase
turning in my hands
til the surface blushed

and my fingers, like flares
and you, Isabella, fruit of youth,
your glowing lips, a flute
blew fire in my mouth

and my body of thin snow
melted under your dark sky

# The Last Road Trip of the Monte Carlo
Jeff Burt

A car can be a church, a place of prayer; a place of rest and repair; a place for steering wheel thumping and loud off-key singing to vent the magma of the soul; a place of revelation between lovers, parent, and child; a place of secreting snacks you don't want others to see you eat; a place of conveying truth to one's self when the home won't do; a place of exorcism, an immune system warding off boredom, insomnia, weariness, and voodoo. The bright green 73 Monte Carlo had been all of these. Except for the voodoo.

My son Ben and I had removed all of our belongings to air it out. We had been on the road for twelve days collecting dust and grit from each state from California to Florida, and an odor not rank but accumulated, part Southwestern, part Texan, part Creole, part the peculiar humidity of the Panhandle. I had taken out the bucket, filled it with water and a minuscule bottle of detergent, and was bathing it down in strokes more appropriate for a horse. Ben checked the mileage and estimated the Monte Carlo had achieved twelve miles per gallon while cruising at near eighty miles per hour the entire way from the Panhandle through lower Alabama, and the Carlo's suspension made it seem the road moved beneath us instead of we over it. Ben swiveled the seats out and swept as best he could the exposed areas, delivering a little bit of Texas, Louisiana, Mississippi, and Florida to the Alabama soil.

The Carlo, as we called it, was an original purchase in 1973 in Omaha, Nebraska. With a big engine, the two-tone green body with the white top, swivel seats in the front, and a glide suspension, it was made for touring.

My service friends and I had used it on numerous road trips, usually on long weekends. We had climbed Pike's Peak in

Colorado, delivered by the Carlo to its base, and used it as an ambulance when Mo got sunstroke and we shaped a makeshift litter and dragged him slowly down the mountain until we could use the Carlo to transport him. We had cruised the Black Hills of South Dakota and gone ninety miles an hour on I-90 until a sudden rainstorm had reduced our speed to a reckless five miles an hour. Lightning had surrounded us, and shortly after the storm passed, a great cloud of grasshoppers encircled the car, smashing into every front-facing inch of the vehicle such that we actually had to scrape the dead insects from the grill and hood and window after a few miles.

We had gone fishing in Arkansas and Missouri, and on one daring long weekend had cruised non-stop to Manhattan to see Dougie's sister for about eight hours in the middle of the night and cruised back to base, with a short stop outside of Cleveland for the Best Omelet South of Lake Erie, a 3000-mile trip in seventy-two hours. Resonating in the floorboards and sidewalls were our stories of stupid sports plays, drinking, failed womanizing, conservative parents, and deep longings to go back home to those same conservative parents.

I had kept the Carlo in the beginning because I could not afford another car, but as it aged, I had become more attached to it. When I married, my wife encouraged me to keep it polished and running, and it became like a pet.

Now, fifty-seven, I was out of work in the new economy, and suddenly age, experience, mastery did not account for anything; certification and a second language accounted for everything. We had already sold our house and moved into an apartment, and the Carlo was the last asset we had to cover our bills. My wife had purchased an all-electric Volt out of the inheritance from her mother's passing. Before I would sell the Carlo, I wanted one last road trip, the last grand tour of the internal combustion engine. Ben was recovering from a broken shoulder that put him on short-term disability, and he had never been west of Nevada and Arizona, so we got a burr under our saddles one night and hit the road two days later.

Before we left, we tuned the carburetor, checked the plugs, and changed the oil by ourselves. Ben took great pleasure in being able to sit on the fender and have a place for his feet in the engine well, and had fun adjusting the carburetor and, despite having the broken shoulder, helped change the plugs. He liked being a mechanic, for once, enjoyed the physical labor, as opposed to his I-phone globally networked and his computer, on which he earned his livelihood. Modern cars certainly run better and more efficiently and safer with the engineers designing all of the controls, but a person takes great joy in being the master mechanic of a car, even if nothing more than tuning a carburetor with a screwdriver to make it roar and backing it off so that the engine purrs so softly the metal does not vibrate. The Monte Carlo does not belong to the Shock and Awe Generation, but as Ben played with settings, drivers, and wrenches, I could see a joy, curiosity, and simple pride of mastery that had nothing to do with intellect come over him. This was not man over machine, not brain over machine. Perhaps this last continental grand tour of the internal combustion engine was the last tour of man and machine in concert, as well.

We cruised westward, back on Highway 98, until Pensacola Bay, and then north to Interstate 110. We stopped in Pensacola for lunch and decided that since we were heading north, this was our last chance for Gulf Coast food, and stopped in a place aptly named The Fish House. The server was more southern than we wanted, greeting us with "Honey" and "Sweetheart."She recommended the crab, and we eagerly dug in, with a bowl of seafood curry and rice on the side, and finished with orange sherbet.

Ben drove, and I slept on the way to Mobile, not more than a half-hour ride.

We traveled north until we hit a detour to the west to the little crossroads, population 208. But as soon as we entered the outskirts, the outskirts being two houses close together on the same side of the street and a large post-World War II Quonset hut. The triangular park by the cemetery, the river quay pier, the city building, the library, the town clock tower—all had been donated by George and Wendell Winston, twin brothers who had entered the Air Force, when I met them, at eighteen in 1971. They left the service in 1975 with an idea on how to improve magnetic recording to media, patented it, marketed it, and by 1980 were reaping six-figure royalties.

They did not go on inventing. Wendell graduated in literature, and for a time, imagined himself as a novelist but hit his stride as a ghostwriter for a successful police procedural series based on a Puritan primer. He called himself a hack, but he was actually a great mimic of the written word and was never without work. He supported his three wives, serially, quite well.

Wendell had left a message at our motel about a voodoo spell. He wanted to see Ben and me that afternoon and sent us a Google map to his estate. It stood about one hundred yards from the road with magnolias lining the drive of crushed white gravel, which looks pretty from a distance but gives off a glare that burns right through sunglasses. The house was a two-story mansion with a screened-in porch on the first story going all the way around the house except on the north side, which was open to a magnificent garden with a few frog ponds and reeds popping up out of the manicured flowerbeds.

Wendell had seen us drive up and was already in the driveway when we stopped. He did not look well. His handshake proved it, feeble and clammy. We said a few pleasantries, and then his ten-year-old son grabbed Ben to shoot hoops, and we were alone. He quietly told me he thought he was slowly being poisoned by his third wife, who still lived in the house even though they were divorced.

"She's Dominican, like the republic. Certainly not like the nuns, though she does have a little bit of the same harshness.

She gets half of my estate when I die. My son gets the other half. Don't ask me why she still lives here and gets what she does when we are divorced. It's all very complicated. But I think she has no patience for death and wants it to hurry up."

"Have you been to a doctor?"

"Yes, secretly. They have found nothing abnormal, but she is quite an herbalist, a gardener. And a witch. And I think she knows how to brew things so that they will produce, you know, poison. Why, we have pennyroyal planted in the garden. The stuff used to abort fetuses, and who knows what that pennyroyal will do in small quantities over time. Who knows."

"Have you talked to the police or a private eye?"

"The police? Please. I know John Russell personally. He has been my best man twice. He's trained in criminal justice, has a master's degree from Auburn. A friend. An educated black man that knows blacks and whites and Hispanics. But he is, after all, a cop, and cops don't do anything without proof. And I have no proof."

"Is this why you wanted me to stop by? You want my help in this?"

"No, no, no," he said dismissively, waving his hand like a fan in front of me. "I wanted to see that Monte Carlo of yours. Brings back many memories. Not all good, mind you. But some good. You remember when we went to that rose garden overlooking the Missouri River, and we were double-dating, and my date Evelyn liked you better and your date Kay liked me better, and we swapped mid-kissing. And you had never kissed a black girl, and I had never kissed a white girl. You forgot the beer, but we had a wonderful time without it. Remember?"

"Yeah, they used the same lipstick, so when you shut your eyes, it didn't seem to matter who was kissing anyway. You just wanted to be kissing. Do you want to go look at the car?"

Wendell stood up uneasily. "I'll get someone to open the garage, and you can park it in there. I can't be out in the sun but five seconds, and my skin boils cuz of the poison."

I walked out to the Carlo and waited until the garage, another two-story structure that could house up to six vehicles, opened, and a young man waved for me to drive up. When I shut off the engine, I introduced myself, and he said nothing but "Roberto."

Wendell came out and didn't talk but ran his hands over the white roof and the fenders. He took the keys from my hand, sat in the driver's seat, started the engine, and revved it a few times, smiling with each push on the accelerator. And then he shut the engine off, gave back my keys, and went back inside. "I can die now," he said, rubbing me the same way he had rubbed the top of the Carlo.

After he had stepped out of the garage, his helper Roberto said, "He's not right, you know. It's cancer."

"He didn't tell me he had cancer. He thinks he is being poisoned."

"He's lost it. It's inoperable brain cancer. He's got about two months left to live."

"He told me he thought his third wife was poisoning him."

Roberto broke in. "He thinks his third wife is poisoning him, but she has not been around for four years. She disappeared and took over three hundred thousand dollars, and no one has seen her since. She was from the Dominican Republic, and everyone thinks she went back, started a new life."

I had my mouth open and decided I should close it.

"Isn't that her son?" I said, gesturing to a boy out on the lawn with a soccer ball.

"Yes, but you know how it is. Mr. Winston, he was quiet and stuck in books all the time, and the rest of the time, he played with his boy. But the mother, she had no time for the boy. His cousin comes by, and she helps with the boy."

"What about his brother George?"

Roberto snorted. "He's a bastard. Wendell can't die quick enough for him. He thinks he will manage the estate. Like a piece of art."

"Who will get the boy?"

"Wendell read us the will. The boy goes to his cousin. The house, too. She will come to live in it."

"Wendell told me that his third wife will get 50 percent."

"No, she gets nothing. He still thinks she is alive in the house somewhere and won't come to see him."

"And does the gardening as well."

Roberto laughed. "The gardening is done by a soft-spoken Mexican who is very handsome. Me."

Ben and I looked over the map to chart our way to Memphis, but with a little side trip into Mississippi to see another old friend who had lost his house in Hurricane Katrina. He was a CPA in Jackson and had married his second cousin when she was fourteen at the time. She had not been pregnant, and indeed, never did get pregnant. They were childless.

I asked to see Wendell, to say goodbye, but he was already back in bed and fast asleep. Ben was kicking a soccer ball with Wendell's son and making him chase all over the lawn for it, which the boy did eagerly like a retriever.

We got in the Monte Carlo, and as I slipped into the seat, a shooting pain traveled from my lower lumbar to my neck, and I knew I would be sitting sidesaddle on the road to Memphis. A second and third pain broke like lightning. As Ben prepared to guide the Carlo down the aisles of magnolias, I adjusted my side mirror, and on the second story of the house, in the last window on the south side, I could see a woman about fifty watching us leave.

She appeared to have a doll in her left hand, and in the right, a very large needle.

# Bijou
## Mary Donaldson-Evans

We should have known better. We were planning a trip through the south of France in the summer of 1991, and we happened to mention to Jean Duprès, a friend of ours, that we would be renting a car. A southern Frenchman, Monsieur Duprès insisted that we allow him to lend us his automobile for our travels. He was in a convalescent center in the town of Hyères, on the Mediterranean coast, and would be unable to drive.

"*Non, non, ça va,*" we protested. We'll be fine with a rental.

"*J'insiste!*" he replied.

His arguments were compelling. Why should we pay for something that he was offering us for nothing? He had no immediate need for the car; it was sitting idle on his property, a sprawling vineyard near the town of Salernes, in southeastern France. He would see that the car was delivered to him in Hyères by the caretaker of his property, Ahmad, and we would pick it up there. All we had to do was to get ourselves to Hyères.

Furthermore, he would arrange for us to be met at the train station by a friend of his. What could be simpler?

Against our better judgment—for who would want the responsibility of a friend's car for travel in a foreign country, when a rental car could be procured at a reasonable price?—we acquiesced. My husband, our fifteen-year-old son, and I flew to Paris in July and, after spending several days in the capital, took a mid-morning train to Toulon from the Gare de Lyon. The trip lasted just over four hours. Madame X met our train and chatted amicably with us as she drove us to the home in Hyères, where Monsieur Duprès was recuperating from a fall.

We were moved to see our dear old friend in a wheelchair, but he was his jovial self, and we relaxed for a long time on the sun-dappled terrace of the "Centre de Gérontologie," sipping mint tea and reminiscing.

In France, which has double daylight savings time, the summer days are long and lazy. Nevertheless, at some point, we realized that we should be getting on our way, as we had hotel reservations in Orange, a mid-sized city some 198 kilometers (approximately 123 miles) to the north of Hyères. Estimating travel time to be just over two hours, we lingered only long enough to collect the car's papers from Monsieur Duprès and to go over our agreement once again: we were to return the car to Salernes in three weeks, at the conclusion of our travels, by which time Monsieur Duprès would have been discharged from the convalescent home. Pushing Monsieur Duprès in his wheelchair, we moved slowly towards the automobile, an Italian Lancia parked just a few yards away. As we approached her, we took the full measure of her condition. Her gunmetal grey paint was dull and pockmarked with rust; the cable attaching the driver's side mirror to the car was reinforced with duct tape; the front fender tilted at an odd angle as if it had been damaged in an accident and repaired by a budget body shop. Seeing our scarcely veiled dismay, Monsieur Duprès assured us that the car had recently passed inspection. He handed us the keys. Was it my imagination, or did he have tears in his eyes as we took possession of his beloved old automobile?

Our first surprise, when we attempted to get into the car, was that we couldn't. Well, that is to say, we couldn't all enter the car in the normal manner, because the front door on the passenger side would not open. Monsieur Duprès laughed sheepishly and explained that the door had not been functional for quite some time and that the front seat passenger—in this case, me—would have to enter the car through the driver's side. We were none too thrilled about this, but we reasoned that the non-opening door did not really affect the car's safety. We loaded our bags into the trunk, and our son Andrew got into a back seat littered with straw. (I didn't ask.) I entered the car on the driver's side, squeezed behind the steering wheel, and slid into the passenger seat.

After acquainting himself with the dashboard, my husband Lance turned the key in the ignition, and the motor roared to life. "Bon voyage!" shouted Monsieur Duprès. And off we went, waving affectionately to our kind old friend.

There was no GPS to guide us in the 1990s. Nevertheless, we found our way to the autoroute quite easily with the aid of a trusted Michelin road map. We had decided that we would stop for dinner at about the mid-point of our journey, near Aix-en-Provence, and we came upon a roadside rest stop just as our stomachs were beginning to rumble. The sun was slowly sinking in the western sky, so we decided we'd better locate the headlight switch before entering the restaurant. Lance pulled on a likely knob. It came off in his hand. He replaced it, pushed it in, tried gently pulling it. Nothing happened.

"Look, let's just get some take-out and be on our way. The sun hasn't set yet," said I.

"But…but…" objected Lance.

I won the argument. We ordered sandwiches to go and then climbed back into our car.

Now then, where were the headlights? One by one, Lance tried every other knob on the dashboard. The steering column had a few levers. These activated the turn signal, windshield wipers, and washers. Finally, he discovered a small knob in an inconspicuous place: the four-way flashers! At least they could provide some illumination should darkness fall before we reached our destination. Better than nothing!

We started out, driving as fast as we dared in order to beat the setting sun. Traffic was blessedly light, and for a while, the sun seemed to hover above the horizon. We willed it to stop its descent. However, when other drivers began to flash their lights at us in an attempt to let us know we needed to put our headlights on, and when we ourselves could not see more than a couple of yards—sorry, meters—in front of the car, we knew it was time to use the four-way flashers. We turned them on and pulled into the right lane, reducing our speed. For the next 45 minutes, we scarcely spoke to one another, so focused were we on the road. Lance's knuckles were white on the steering wheel; I felt my mouth go dry. All of the muscles in our body were tense. Each time a car passed us on the left, we had an adrenalin rush, caught in the grip of doubt: could they see us clearly? We heaved a sigh of relief when we found ourselves once again alone on the highway.

Even our son Andrew had fallen silent.

Before this, we'd always enjoyed driving in Europe, where kilometers went by so much more quickly than miles. Now, however, given our slow speed, the kilometer markings seemed maddeningly far apart. The four-way flashers seemed to flicker at times. What if they went out altogether? We banished that thought from our minds. The darker it got, the more slowly we drove.

Not so slowly, however, that we didn't manage to miss the exit ramp for Orange. How did we do that?! By this time, Lance's foot was doing a jig on the accelerator, and I was feeling almost nauseated with fear. Andrew suddenly came alive in the back seat. Typical teenager that he was, he exulted at the stupidity of his parents. He laughed—yes, laughed—when he discovered we had missed the exit.

Somehow, we succeeded in exiting the freeway and in finding our way back into Orange. The hotel, a chambre d'hôte (similar to a B & B), was centrally located, and we heaved a huge sigh of relief when we felt the gravel of the hotel drive beneath our tires. We had arrived! We didn't worry unduly about the headlights: we'd have plenty of time the following day to take the car to a Lancia dealer and get instructions as to how to operate them.

We checked in and fell exhausted into bed.

The following day, after a leisurely breakfast of fresh baguettes, flaky croissants, and strong coffee, we asked the hotel proprietress for directions to the nearest Lancia dealership. Lance was once again at the wheel when we set off, but it wasn't more than ten minutes before the steering wheel itself ceased to function properly. That is to say, it ceased to act the way steering wheels should. It was as if it had become disconnected from the wheels, spinning through his hands in either direction. We gasped! Thank God the brakes still worked!

I cannot tell you how we managed to get to the Lancia repair shop. The steering wheel somehow "engaged" every now and then, allowing us to make turns. Divine intervention most certainly played a role, of that we were sure. Anyway, there we were, attempting to explain to the mechanic what had happened. He'd look at it, no problem. Come back in a couple of hours.

We had envisioned spending our time in Orange visiting the Triumphal Arch and the Museum of Art and History, enjoying a wine tasting at the Château de Beaucastel, strolling through the Orange Cathedral. We had *not* expected to spend two hours killing time at a downscale shopping center while our Lancia was being examined and diagnosed. When, finally, we returned to the service station, the mechanic emerged from the garage, shaking his head as he wiped his hands on a greasy rag. Behind and above him, we spied the Lancia, elevated on a hydraulic lift, looking most undignified.

"Désolé," he said. Your car is unsafe. I cannot let you drive it away.

What? We were incredulous. How much would it cost to repair?

"Trop," he replied. Too much. "To be honest, the car is not worth salvaging. It should be sold for scrap metal."

We thought our French was relatively fluent. However, truth be told, it was confined to more everyday subjects that did not include axles and gears, driving shafts and steering columns. We thus listened in utter confusion as the mechanic attempted to explain to us just what was ailing our old car. "*La plume de ma tante / est sur le bureau de mon oncle*," did not begin to bridge the gulf of incomprehension that divided us. We shrugged, left the keys and the car with him, and called a taxi.

Back at our hotel, we went about making phone calls to

car rental agencies. Because this was a last-minute rental, we could not take advantage of the discounts that would have been available to us had we rented a car two months in advance through Europcar, as we had originally intended to do. At long last, we found a suitable car and Lance went to fetch it.

We loaded the trunk and prepared to leave.

But there was one more thing we had to do before setting off. We had to phone Monsieur Duprès and explain the whole, sad story to him.

"You call," said Lance.

"No, you call," said I. "I'm not the one who practically shares a name with the car."

"But I'm not the one who made friends with Monsieur Duprès in the first place," retorted Lance.

We flipped a one-franc coin (the Euro didn't exist in 1991). "Heads you win, tails you lose," said Lance.

It came up tails.

I dialed Monsieur Duprès's number. He answered on the first ring.

I summoned my best French to explain what had happened.

The car had broken down, it was unsafe to drive, and—*je suis vraiment désolée*—we would not be able to return it to him in Salernes.

"Quoi?!" Monsieur Duprès was devastated, for us, of course, but also for his poor old car.

His voice trembling with emotion, he explained that this was not just any old car. He had given it to his late wife for one of her last birthdays, and together they had named it "Bijou" (Jewel). The car may have been a worthless piece of junk, but it had great sentimental value for Monsieur Duprès, a *bijou* in every sense of the word. The thought that he would never again see it was unbearable to him. Distressed by the depth of his anguish, I felt my heart clench with pity. I expressed my condolences, then gave him the name and phone number of the Lancia dealership.

Convinced that Monsieur Duprès would realize the car's

damage was irreparable, saddened by this turn of events but feeling no responsibility and thus no guilt, we continued with our road trip through France, turned in our rental car unscathed, and flew home. We wasted no time in writing to our kind old friend to thank him for his generous gesture and to reiterate our regret that things had not turned out as we had expected them to. Imagine our surprise a few weeks later when we learned that Monsieur Duprès had indeed paid to have "Bijou" repaired (no doubt for a princely sum but he was too discreet to reveal it) and that Ahmad had taken the train to Orange to fetch it. The old car was now back "home," and except for the front passenger door, which still would not open, it was in perfect condition. "*Même les phares marchent!*" (even the headlights work!) exulted Monsieur Duprès, obviously thrilled that his moribund old friend had been resurrected.

Monsieur Duprès himself, on the other hand, was in declining health, and we never saw him again. Some four years later, Ahmad wrote to us to tell us of the old gentleman's passing. We were deeply touched to have been informed, and the following year, when we returned to France, we made a special trip to Salernes to say hello to Ahmad. As our car bounced along the rutted road that led to Monsieur Duprès's charming old farmhouse, we were surprised to see Bijou, parked just a few meters from the house, looking every bit as run down as she had looked when we first laid eyes on her.

Ahmad welcomed us warmly and treated us to a sumptuous Moroccan meal in "*L'Etoile du sud*," the restaurant he had set up in a tent on the property. Afterward, we chatted over coffee as thick as mud, and we mentioned Bijou, expressing our astonishment that the car was still there.

Ahmad smiled sadly. "Ah, but I cannot get rid of it." He seemed disinclined to explain, but our curiosity got the best of us, and we begged to know why.

In a voice that was choked with emotion, Ahmad confessed that he had done something "terrible." He beckoned us to follow him to the car, and he opened one of the rear doors.

There, on the floor mat behind the driver's seat, was a gritty substance, grey in color, sandy in texture. "*Qu'est-ce que c'est?*" we asked. What is it?

"*Hélas, ce sont les cendres de Monsieur Duprès,*" he explained. He had been transporting his master's ashes for burial in the far reaches of the vineyard when the urn tipped over and the ashes spilled out. What could he do? He could hardly sell the car in that condition.

And it would be sacrilegious to attempt to vacuum the ashes out. He shuddered.

We didn't know whether to laugh or cry. Ahmad, who was like a son to Monsieur Duprès, was truly upset. We sympathized. But then we reflected on our history with old Bijou, and we saw the humor in her current situation. That decrepit old jalopy had given new meaning to the adage "No good deed goes unpunished." Whereas the punishment usually befalls the do-gooder, in our case, both the good Samaritan— Monsieur Duprès—and we, the beneficiaries of his kindness, were punished. And now here she was, home on the vineyard, cared for like a precious relic. Once a memorial to Madame Duprès, Bijou had been repurposed as the mausoleum of Monsieur Duprès. To think we had once believed her to be beyond help! Had she been endowed with the gift of language, dear Bijou might have said, with Mark Twain, "Reports of my death have been greatly exaggerated."

As we took our leave of Ahmad, we cast a backward glance at Bijou and committed her, not to the junk heap of wrecked cars but to our memory, where she will live on, rust to rust, ashes to ashes.

# Sometimes Town
## Richard Luftig

The sign announcing its name
as you enter says the population
is almost a thousand. If so,
then four hundred folks were on
vacation when the last census occurred.
But no matter. It still holds the title

of birthplace of that famous poet—
no matter that no one quite remembers
his name, and they claimed the guy
a full ten years before he was born.
This place where the only thing
growing is the number of once-farm

fields now reduced to bunch grass
and thistle, where winds out
of the northwest blow so hard
against this flat land that snow
moves sideways like it never intends
to touch the Earth. But you know

it does. Here, where people
take pride that three inches
can fall at midnight and by nine
in the morning there still won't
be a single set of tire tracks
on the two-lane. Where the bet

of the day is whether the mail
truck will make it out to roads

named after families who live
here six generations after their ancestors
settled and broke the soil. This on-again,
off-again, sometimes town where we need

the noon farm report on the local radio
to remind us that we are still here,
and how folks who live in the houses
along the lone road that runs through
this town are more important than anything
that might ever take place at its end.

# Liar's Table
## Richard Luftig

About the only thing genuine
in this place is the coffee
and even then if I ask
the waitress if it's fresh
she says, *Define fresh.*

So, I rephrase the question:
*Ok, then, when was it brewed,*
and one of the guys at the Liar's Table
says, *What month is it?*
I asked once if the chile

was spicy and was told I had
to get a waiver from the cook.
It's been this way for thirty years:
us widowers with no place better to go,
there before first wink of sunlight,

waiting for the place to open.
One of us grabs the morning paper
from behind the register
then we move to our table that no one
is allowed to sit at without us taking a vote.

Marty, who has probably never
been east of Indiana in his life
sports his ratty sea-captain cap,
and Dave tells the same story
about how some poor guy

wandered in for directions
to the next town only to end up
driving two counties out of his way.
Then we take bets over which tourist
will bend to pick up the quarter

we've super-glued to the sidewalk
in front of the restaurant window.
Still, maybe the best thing about lying
is that the facts aren't really expected
to add up and you can't prove a negative,

like when we tell the same stories
about daughters who call us each evening
to see how we are or sons who ask
us to live with them and say they will
be coming to get us sometime soon.

# Hotel
## Tim Frank

The hotel flickered on the edge of the city like a TV channel tuning in and out of focus. It appeared against the horizon beyond the skyscrapers and blocks of flats, the lights from bedrooms stacked floor above floor, standing tall amongst the roads that snaked around it. Planes cruised by the building, but the blasts of turbines were a faint hiss from where Joseph stood on the main street, waiting impatiently for his cab.

Finally, his ride pulled up—the driver wound down his window and gave a serene, toothy smile, dried mayonnaise smudged across his week-old stubble.

"I'm Andre," the driver said, stepping out and taking hold of Joseph's suitcase.

Joseph yanked it back. "I'd rather keep hold of this, if it's all the same."

Andre held up his hands.

Once they were both inside the car, Andre asked, "So, where to, chum?"

Joseph leaned forward and pointed at the hotel, flashing like a mirage across the city.

"Well, never been there," said Andre, "but we just need to get across the spaghetti junction, and we shall arrive. Piece of cake."

Andre gently accelerated away and glided into the flow of traffic.

"Let me introduce you to the sprogs." Andre pointed at some mugshots of his children. "Alan, Davey, and the little one, with the yellow bow, is Savanna. She's the apple of my eye."

"Lovely," said Joseph.

"You got any kids, buddy?"

"That's... unimportant."

"Sure, sure. You seem the quiet type. So... silence, I guess."

Andre picked from a Caesar salad resting in a Tupperware pot on the passenger seat.

"Please hurry, I have an urgent meeting to attend," said Joseph.

Listen, everyone wants to get somewhere. I do, you do. Please, just relax, and we'll get there."

A moment passed, and Andre said, "What's this meeting about anyway, buddy?"

Joseph clutched his bag tight and mumbled the words, "Um, fashion convention."

Andre sped onto the spaghetti junction, then swerved as a pigeon fluttered above the windscreen. "Stay calm," he said to himself and the road.

"Excuse me, but are those wild mushrooms in your salad?" Joseph said.

"I picked them myself," Andre said proudly.

"How lovely. I used to forage for them as a child. May I try one?"

"Of course, be my guest."

Joseph scooped up a few and gobbled them whole.

Andre raised a finger to his lips. "Quick question: are you on any kind of medication?"

"Why?" said Joseph, having opened his pillbox and knocked back handfuls of antipsychotics.

"No reason," Andre said innocently. "But just so you know, the mushrooms you ate are kinda, well, magical."

"What are you saying? You spiked me?" Joseph cried.

"Well, I didn't exactly spike you. You just ate them."

"Oh, this is not good, not good at all. Wait, turn here. Here!"

"That wasn't the turning. Don't worry; I have it all in hand. Allow the peace and love."

"Look what you've done. Now we have to go all the way around again."

Andre pulled over onto the hard shoulder and swiveled to face Joseph, whose eyes were beginning to bulge.

"Let me explain a few things about me, my background, and how I run this cab. Firstly, if you ingest any hallucinogenic in this vehicle, then that's your responsibility. Secondly, this is a family space, hence the photos. My family is always with me in spirit, and that brings me to my third, final, and most important point; my car is a haven for tranquility. So, basically, I'm going to need you to relax."

"Look, cut the shit, just get me to the hotel. I can still make it in time. God, if only you used sat-nav."

Andre seethed. "I know the way. I always know the way."

Joseph popped a couple more pills to tide him over as the edges of his mind unraveled, and things became a little planetary.

An hour later, night had wrapped itself around the sky. Cars illuminated the motorway like spotlights in a theatre.

"Stop," ordered Joseph, drool oozing down his chin. He kept digging in his suitcase and swallowing panels of pharmaceuticals. "I can walk to the hotel from here."

"What are you talking about? It's still miles away."

"I see it! It's right there!"

Andre hit the brakes, halting in the middle of the road. Cars honked furiously. He wasn't fazed. He got out and dragged Joseph from the backseat, hurling him toward the safety barrier. Joseph's suitcase split open, and clothes spread everywhere across the uneven gravel. There were bras, tights, corsets, high heels, blouses, and miniskirts scattered across the weeds. Joseph held back tears as he scrambled to retrieve his clothes.

"Fashion convention, huh?" said Andre.

"Look away, look away!" Joseph said.

"Oh, look, I'm sorry, okay? What do I care if you wear women's clothes?"

"Leave me alone now. Please. I can get to the hotel from here."

"Do you see any hotel?" Andre said, grabbing Joseph by the collar, pointing to an empty skyline.

"Wait," said Joseph, "I swear it was there."

Both men scoured the panorama, but the hotel was nowhere to be seen.

"Where have you taken me?" Andre said, up close to Joseph's face.

Joseph locked his suitcase.

"Thought you were a man of compassion," Joseph sulked.

"Oh, the family spirit?" Andre said, feeling all his extremities vividly. "Those kids aren't mine. Ripped them out of a magazine. I'm a recovering addict. Godamn these shrooms. They haunt me!"

"I was fine before I met you," Joseph said.

"Same here."

Then, silence.

"Wait, is that the hotel, over there, looking so alive and underwater?" said Andre.

"I think so."

"It's beautiful—the light, its aura."

"Can we go?"

"Yes, I think we should."

The hotel was glowing like a manifested jewel, and they would reach it, no matter what their differences. After all, it was just so close.

# Corncob Caper
## Bruce Harris

Each year, the cheap New York City hotel rooms became seedier, people nastier, and the pipe-selling business tougher. Not that there were any fewer pipe smokers around. In fact, just the opposite. If nothing else, Bill Ballentine was a salesman who did his homework. Pipe smokers have increased by at least ten percent every year since the war. There were a lot more potential customers to reach since Ballentine entered the racket in 1941. Of course, more customers brought more competition. Aggressive competition.

Ballentine inched his way through the ill-lit hallway back to room 5, clutching the too-small towel around his waist. The bath felt good after the long journey from Albany. He unlocked the door and tossed the towel onto the bed. He shaved in the room, put on a tie and sports jacket, and thought about his plan of attack. He'd visit four stores, beginning with Pete's Pipe Place in the Piermont Building and finishing at Skyline Tobacco near his Times Square flop. This New York selling trip was going to be a little different. Ballentine brought with him a line of corncob pipes. His boss, Mr. Brunton, laughed at the idea.

"Are you nuts, Ballentine?" he yelled. "There ain't no such thing as city hicks. You ain't gonna sell none of them darn things to them sophisticates."

Ballentine grinned. His sales skills were put to the test even before hitting the road. He never did anything spur of the moment, except with his girl, Helen Richardson. He met her in the public library six months ago and had spent all his available time with her. They were crazy about each other. Before his upcoming Manhattan trip, he planned to pop the question.

"I know things, boss," Ballentine answered.

"Great. I got me a salesman who knows things. The only thing you need to know is how to sell pipes. Spend a little less time with that girl…what's her name…."

"Helen."

"Whatever. You're spending too much time with her and not—"

Ballentine heard enough. "I can promise you I'll sell out of these corncobs, and you'll have so many orders you'll have trouble keeping them in stock."

"And how do you propose to do that, lover boy?" Brunton asked.

"Like I said, I know things. The Farmer Takes a Wife," Ballentine said.

"What? Have you gone crazy, Ballentine?"

"It's a movie. It's scheduled to come out early next year."

Brunton rubbed a fat hand over his bald head. "That's great. I'll be sure to miss it."

Ballentine shook his head. "No, you don't understand. The movie stars Clark Gable and Carole Lombard. Gable plays the farmer. More specifically, a pipe-smoking farmer. And to be even more specific—"

"A corncob pipe smoker farmer?" Brunton asked. His expression was a combination of amused, confused, and intrigued.

"The wife, played by Lombard," Ballentine began, "buys the corncob for Gable. You know what that means? Every woman who sees this movie will have the same idea and buy a corncob for their boyfriend or husband. And every unattached man would—"

Again Brunton finished Ballentine's sentence. "Want to be just like Clark Gable." The boss hesitated. "You know, Ballentine, for the first time, you just might be on to something with this idea. I like it! Just make sure you come back here with no pipes left in your case. Because if you don't, you're fired!"

Brunton's words rattled around in Ballentine's brain as he searched the poky hotel room for the pipes. He remembered placing the leather case containing a dozen corncobs on the dresser. It was gone! Someone had come into his room while he bathed and lifted the pipe case. Ballentine rushed downstairs and slammed the bell on the front desk.

"I'm coming…I'm coming," came the voice from a back room.

After years in sales, Ballentine read people as well as books. "Where are they?" he asked.

"I beg your pardon?" the clerk said.

"The pipes. What'd you do with them?"

The man blinked through thick black frame glasses. "I don't—"

"Look here, mister…." Ballentine let the word hang.

"Mullins."

"Look here, pal. A case of pipes was taken from my room, room 5, while I was taking a bath. But you know all that."

"I can assure you—"

"Save it, Mullins. I locked my room door when I took the bath. That means you are the only one who could have opened it. You either have the pipes or know where they are."

"Is this a joke?" Mullins asked.

"You want a joke? Okay." Ballentine grabbed the clerk by the collar and brought Mullins' face inches from his own. He rested a fist on the clerk's cheek. "I'll send you to the moon, Mullins. Funny, right?" He pulled his fist back as if ready to strike.

"Okay! Okay! Stop," Mullins pleaded.

Ballentine released his grip.

"Truth is," Mullins began, adjusting his collar, "neither is true." The confused, combative expression on Ballentine's face propelled Mullins to continue. "I don't have them, and I don't know where they are," he said.

Ballentine's forward movement caused Mullins to raise both hands in surrender. "I…I…think I can help you," he said.

Ballentine eased off. "You think?"

Mullins looked down. "Okay, I know." He reached into

his back pocket, opened his wallet, and pulled out a twenty. "Here." He slid the note toward Ballentine.

"What's this?" the salesman asked.

"That's what I got for opening your door."

Ballentine was tempted to reach across the counter and drag Mullins over the splintered structure and lay a hard right to his chin. "Talk," was all he said.

Mullins swallowed hard. "Not much to tell. After you checked in, this guy comes up to the desk and gives me the money if I agree to open the door to your room."

"And you just take the money and do it?"

"He said he was a policeman checking for stolen goods." Mullins noticed Ballentine's skin color change. "Okay, so I didn't really believe him. But, the money...my son is sick and—"

"Save it!" Ballentine said. "What did he look like? Where'd he go?"

Mullins shook his head. "I don't know. He wore a mask."

"A what? A mask? A masked policeman?"

Ballentine thought about contacting the real police but decided against it. He couldn't provide any information about the thief, and he didn't want to be bogged down with questions and paperwork. He could turn Mullins in, but that wouldn't bring his pipes back or save his job. He returned to the rat trap that was room 5. *Why would anyone want to steal the pipes?* he thought. For the first time, he checked his own wallet. Nothing missing! The wallet was in his pants pocket on the dresser next to the pipe case. Why would someone enter his room, not take his money, but take his wares instead? It didn't add up. Unless it was one of his competitors. But, who among them knew he was planning a trip to New York City? He started laughing. *A masked cop! Of all the ridiculous...*

Ballentine's brief-lived joviality was forgotten as he headed back downstairs to use the telephone in what the hotel called a lobby and inform his boss about the loss. He was met on the stairs by Mullins. The clerk held an envelope.

"This came for you," Mullins said. "For the gentleman in room 5" was hand-printed on the envelope.

Ballentine took it. "Who brought this? Where did this come from?"

Mullins looked downward. "I don't know."

Ballentine's lips thinned. "You don't know a helluva lot, do you? Another masked cop?"

"I don't know," Brunton repeated. "I...um...stepped out for a moment. When I came back, this," he pointed to the envelope in Ballentine's hand, "was on the counter. I didn't see who left it and didn't notice anyone coming or going. I'm sorry, I—"

"Forget it," Ballentine said. He turned around and returned to the room. He read:

WANT YOUR PIPES? MEET ME TONIGHT—9:00— BENCH AT THE WEST 93RD STREET ENTRANCE TO CENTRAL PARK

———— ✦ ————

Ballentine saw the seated figure as he neared the park. He didn't notice the mask until he got closer to the bench. The pipe case was nowhere in sight. "Police?" he asked.

"Very funny," the man said. "Please, take a seat."

"I'll stand if it's all the same to you," Ballentine said. "Now, do you mind telling me what's this all about? And where are my pipes?" Ballentine didn't recognize the voice. The man's eyes looked familiar, though.

"I don't blame you for being upset," the man said.

"That's nice of you," Ballentine said in his most sarcastic voice.

"I'm working on behalf of someone. The someone is unimportant. Fact is, the someone doesn't even know I'm doing this."

Ballentine thought about ripping the mask off the guy but knew the only thing that would accomplish was to guarantee he'd never recover his pipes. "You're talking in riddles. I repeat, what's this all about, and where are my pipes?"

"The pipes are safe. This is about a business proposition," the man said.

"Keep talking."

The man nodded. "How would you like to make money?" He held up his hand. "I'm talking real money. How much would each of those corncobs normally go for?"

"None of your business," Ballentine said.

The man ignored him. "I can get $25 each. Do the math. A dozen pipes would bring you…bring us…$300. That's a lot of money; more I dare venture to say than you make in a month."

Ballentine shook his head. "Suppose I turn you over to the legit police and report all this."

Again, the man acted as if he didn't hear Ballentine. "Okay, Chang."

Out from the darkness emerged a figure.

"This is Mr. Chang," the masked man began. Chang bowed. "Mr. Chang has himself a little business in Chinatown. You and I, Ballentine, don't need to concern ourselves much with Mr. Chang's line of work. It involves opium and –"

"Say, what is all this?" Ballentine asked.

"Like I was saying, the two of us have nothing to do with that. But, Mr. Chang here really wants the corncob pipes for his line of work, and he's willing to pay the already quoted price…in cash. All you have to do is agree. We get paid, and we never see each other or Mr. Chang again."

Ballentine looked from one to the other before focusing on the pipe thief. "Let me ask you this, why did you bring me out here? If you wanted to sell the pipes to him, you could have done it without me."

The man jerked a nail-bitten thumb in Chang's direction. "Him."

Chang bowed again.

The man continued, "I made the mistake of telling him how I…um…acquired the pipes. He didn't like that. Some

Chinatown way of doing business that I'll never understand. He said you are the rightful owner and must share in the profits for the deal to occur. So, here we all are. Decide. We don't have all night."

"I've decided," Ballentine said. "I'm reporting both of you to the police."

For the first time, the man stood. "That won't be necessary, Bill." He removed his mask. Ballentine didn't recognize the man, but like the eyes, it seemed as though Ballentine had seen a similar face before.

"I think it's time we were properly introduced. This is my good friend, Harry Park." Park, alias Chang, grinned and bowed. "Forgive me for giving him a false name. I didn't want to take any chances."

"Chances about what?" Ballentine asked.

"My sister's future. My name is Phil Richardson. I'm Helen's brother."

Ballentine's jaw dropped. "You're Helen's…" but he didn't finish his thought. Now that he knew, he saw the resemblance.

"That's right," Richardson said. "I'm the only thing in this world Helen had until she met you. Forgive my over-protectiveness of her. When she told me you asked to marry her, she was so excited. I just had to do something to make sure of your character. You know that you're the right guy— an honest guy with some scruples. I can't have my little sister marry just anybody. I guess you'll do." Richardson and Park/Chang bowed.

# La Tour sans Argent
## Mary Donaldson-Evans

True story: My son and his friend walked out of a Michelin-starred restaurant in Paris after a sumptuous three-course lunch...without spending a single euro.

It happened in the spring of 2001, when my husband and I were in Paris directing a study-abroad program. This was a transitional period for France's currency, and the franc was still accepted as legal tender. Not that this is particularly relevant, because the kids didn't spend a single franc either.

As classmates in the University of Pennsylvania's graduate program in architecture, Andrew and Kelly had both applied for summer grants that would enable them to travel throughout France, studying its architectural marvels and sketching and photographing them. Both were awarded small scholarships. In Kelly's case, the benefactor who had funded her travel grant flew her to Texas so that he could meet her. She mentioned that she would be spending time in Paris.

"Great!" enthused her benefactor. "You must have lunch or dinner at la Tour d'Argent. Claude Terrail, the owner, is a personal friend of mine. He'll take good care of you."

"Does that mean he'll comp the meal?" asked Andrew, more than a little impressed by the 105 euro prix fixe lunch that was listed on the restaurant's website. Kelly had invited him to join her, and he didn't want any unpleasant surprises.

"Of course! What else could it mean?" replied Kelly.

"Well, it's not certain what 'he'll take good care of you' means," objected Andrew.

"Look, Mr. X knows how that our grants are modest. Would he suggest that I eat at a pricey restaurant if he thought the money would come out of the grant?"

Andrew conceded.

Four months later, they were in Paris, Andrew staying with my husband and me in an apartment on the rue d'Hauteville, Kelly in an inexpensive hotel in the Quartier Latin. They used the phone in our apartment to make lunch reservations, tingling with pleasure at the thought that they would soon be dining in one of the world's most famous restaurants, and what's more, a restaurant with a delicious pun in its name, "Tour d'argent" meaning both "tower of money" and "silver tower."

The following Thursday, they found themselves walking towards a small round table set with sterling silver plates and goblets, candlesticks, cutlery placed with impeccable precision on an ivory linen tablecloth. The tuxedoed maître d' who had shown them to their table stood discreetly to the side as they settled into the cane-backed dining chairs with blue plush seats.

The menu was presented with a flourish, and they studied it carefully. Having done their homework in advance, Andrew and Kelly knew that the restaurant's signature dish was its pressed duck, and so, for the main course, they ordered duckling for two, excited to be getting a certificate with the number of their duck. For the first course, they had to decide among *caviar maison, foie gras roi des Trois Empereurs*, and *pâté en croûte*: Kelly went for the caviar; Andrew decided on the pâté in a pastry crust. For dessert, Kelly was tempted by the crêpes "mademoiselle" while Andrew went for the baba with Tour d'Argent champagne. The sommelier recommended a glass of crisp Pouilly-Fuissé to accompany the caviar, and for Andrew, a Fleurie for the country pâté. A bottle of Côtes de Nuit Village would be a good pairing with the canard à la presse. Andrew realized that the wine steward was suggesting something that he thought would be in their budget, and in a display of bravado that was not really typical of his behavior, he summoned his best French to say to the man: "*D'accord. Mais quel est le meilleur vin pour accompagner le canard à la presse?*"

The best wine for this gourmet dish? The sommelier

looked at him and hesitated. But he had been asked for a recommendation, and he was only too happy to make a suggestion. He turned the pages of the wine list, as thick as a phone book, and pointed:

Chambertin-Clos de Bèze Grand Cru, € 298.

Andrew gulped, and he felt his face flush. He had imagined something in the 50 € range. But wasn't Kelly's benefactor picking up the tab for this meal? This was a once-in-a-lifetime opportunity: why waste it? He also guessed that the wine steward was expecting him to return to the original selection, and he didn't want to give him the satisfaction of being right.

He nodded. "*Très bien.*"

The sommelier bowed and left to fetch the wines.

"Andrew, are you crazy?" Kelly asked as soon as he had left.

"Yep!" he said, with such conviction that they both laughed.

Sighing with the pleasure of anticipation, they leaned back and surveyed their surroundings.

Located on the Quai de la Tournelle, the restaurant looked out on Notre Dame, the storied cathedral on the Ile de la Cité, its flying buttresses glinting in the early afternoon sunlight. The Seine flowed noiselessly below their window, and the trees along the quay were just beginning to sprout the tender green leaves of springtime.

When they turned their attention to the other diners, they were humbled. Even in their best going-out attire, they were keenly aware that they looked like students, worse still, American students. Kelly was wearing black pants and clogs, with a pale blue cashmere pullover; Andrew had his best chinos and a button-down striped shirt topped by a navy blazer. If you didn't look too closely, you didn't realize that his black canvas shoes were, in fact, Nikes. Horrors! Sneakers at the Tour d'Argent!

"Are those the only shoes you have?" Kelly had asked when they met at our apartment before heading out to the restaurant.

"Afraid so. Sorry," said Andrew. "Do you really think anyone will notice?"

"I do," said Kelly. "But never mind. I don't think there's an official dress code for lunch, which means that they won't deny us entry. That's the important thing."

Fortunately, the wine steward and the waiters treated them with such grace and warmth that they put their complexes aside. However, they were more than a little intimidated by the perfectly tailored suits and the stylish dresses of the diners around them.

It wasn't more than ten minutes before a waiter appeared to take their order. A few minutes later, he approached with a silver tray to offer them a complimentary glass of the house champagne to start off their lunch. Another waiter followed with a green asparagus velouté in a ramekin that was scarcely bigger than a thimble, accompanied by a tiny dollop of creamy goat cheese studded with truffle pieces in a mille-feuilles nest. They were in gastronomic heaven, and they had scarcely begun the meal.

"Too bad we're only classmates and not a real couple," laughed Andrew. "You kind of feel you should get engaged, just to do justice to the ambiance."

Kelly joined in the laughter. As she and Andrew were both in committed relationships with other people, they had no interest in each other except as friends.

"But what a friend," thought Andrew, as he sipped his champagne and watched as one of their several waiters quietly placed a crusty little French roll on their side plate. They floated through the meal, savored every bite, marveled at the intriguing blend of textures and flavors, noticing how beautifully the wines they had selected with the wine steward's help complemented the dishes with which they were paired. The duck in its rich dark sauce was even more exquisite when followed with a sip of the Chambertin. *So this is what a 300 euro bottle of wine tastes like*, thought Andrew.

The service was attentive but not overbearing. Andrew and Kelly were sitting back, feeling more than a little buzzed, when glasses of Sauternes were placed on their table along with a small plate of gourmet chocolates and *petits fours*. They clinked their glasses and looked at each other, basking in the euphoria of the moment.

For the first time, Andrew noticed that Kelly had a beautiful smile.

Kelly became aware of Andrew's deep blue eyes.

Over cups of the most flavorful espresso they'd ever tasted, they looked at each other with misty eyes.

The magical moment didn't last because Andrew glanced at his watch and remembered that he'd told my husband and me that he'd be back to the apartment by 3 p.m. It was 2:30. Andrew didn't have a French cell phone, so he couldn't just whip one out of his pocket to alert us to the delay.

They lingered a bit longer, uncertain whether they would be presented with the bill or not, confused as to what they should do.

Having completed servicing their table, the wait staff seemed to have disappeared. Few patrons remained in the dining room.

"It seems obvious that they don't expect us to pay," said Andrew.

"Well, they certainly aren't hovering, waiting for us to ask for the bill," agreed Kelly.

Andrew was the first to dare mention Monsieur Terrail. Putting on his best undergraduate French, he summoned the wine steward and told him that Kelly knew a friend of the restaurant's owner and that she had been asked to greet him.

"Monsieur Terrail?" asked the sommelier. "*Mais il est là en ce moment!*"

He was actually present in the restaurant? At 83 years of age, a restaurateur would not be expected to supervise his kitchen so closely. Kelly and Andrew were ecstatic.

"Perhaps Mr. X told him to watch out for us," speculated Andrew.

"That hardly seems likely," countered Kelly. "After all, the reservation was made in your name."

Scarcely two minutes had passed when they saw a smiling silver-haired gentleman approach their table.

"Mademoiselle Kelly?" he asked, addressing Kelly.

"*Oui*," Kelly gushed, holding out her hand.

And he kissed it! Claude Terrail kissed Kelly's hand!

What followed was a dream come true. This famous restaurant owner, who had countless friends among the rich and famous, who had personally dined in his own restaurant with Ava Gardner, Jayne Mansfield, and other luminaries, whose historic restaurant had been mentioned in novels by Ernest Hemingway and Marcel Proust, this man, Claude Terrail, invited them to tour his famous wine cellar with him.

Opportunities like this didn't come along every day. They accepted eagerly, Andrew without another thought for his time constraints. We'd understand: he was sure of that!

As they walked through the dimly lit wine cellar that prides itself on storage conditions second to none and that boasts of some of the world's most famous vintages, lovingly described in the restaurant's 400-page wine list, they were speechless, so awed were they by what they saw and heard. Terrail explained that the better wines had been walled off to keep them from the Nazis during the Occupation. Among the 320,000 bottles of wine lying there, there were trophy wines, wines that had seen events in French history that they had studied as undergraduates, world-famous wines dating back to 1858.

"That's just one year after *Madame Bovary* was published," whispered Kelly.

"Shhhh...!" hissed Andrew, not wanting to miss a word of what Monsieur Terrail was telling them about a Château d'Yquem dating from 1871.

At the conclusion of the tour, Monsieur Terrail accompanied them to the restaurant entrance and wished them a good day. They thanked him warmly for the tour and turned to face the maître d' and a couple of other uniformed employees standing nearby, waiters they didn't recognize. They all bowed and smiled and sent them on their way.

"*Au revoir, M'sieur-Dame. Merci, M'sieur-Dame. A la prochaine. Bon après-midi!*"

The maître d' opened the door for them.

And they were out! Amazing!

"Do you think we should have left a tip at least?" asked Kelly.

"Oh, I didn't think of that," replied Andrew. "But no, I'm afraid they would have found that insulting."

They looked longingly at the Seine, wishing they had time for a walk along the quays, but Andrew was eager to return to the apartment. Leaving Kelly on the sidewalk, he ducked into a metro.

Meanwhile, back at the apartment on the rue d'Hauteville, the phone was ringing when we returned from grocery shopping on Rue du Faubourg-Saint-Denis. We missed the call. However, when we checked our voice messages, there were three, each one angrier and more frantic than the one before.

The calls were made by the manager of La Tour d'Argent, requesting an immediate call-back.

It did not take a rocket scientist to work out what had happened. My husband picked up the receiver and dialed the number of the restaurant.

"*Bonjour! Tour d'Argent,*" responded a male voice dripping with honey. This was before the era of caller ID.

"*Bonjour, c'est Monsieur Donaldson à l'appareil,*" replied my husband.

We had always found the French language beautiful, melodious and romantic, and devoid of the harsh consonants to be found in, say, German.

The string of invectives that assaulted Lance's ear had nothing beautiful or romantic about it.

Something outrageous had happened.

We had dined in the famous restaurant and had left without paying the bill.

This was *inadmissible!* If the bill were not settled *immédiatement*, the manager would report us to the police. His

160

words burned with anger.

Lance attempted to explain that we were not the offenders, that it was our son who had dined at the Tour d'Argent, and that he would phone them when he returned. This did not satisfy the manager, who continued his angry tirade.

Lance hung up on him.

Twenty minutes later, Andrew arrived.

"How was lunch?" we asked pleasantly.

Andrew launched into a detailed description of the meal, the service, the ambiance, and the wine cellar tour. He waxed positively lyrical as he tried to communicate the sheer bliss of the entire experience.

"And to think it didn't cost us a single euro!" he enthused.

As difficult as it was to break the news to him, we couldn't allow him to labor under the illusion that he'd had a free meal in a two-star restaurant any longer.

"Um...you've had a phone call from La Tour d'Argent," I told him. "They'd like you to call them back. The guy on the phone didn't sound too happy."

Andrew blanched. And then, without further delay—did we raise our kids right or what?—he screwed up his courage and made the call.

Andrew's French comprehension would have been put to the test had he not suspected what the problem would be.

"*Excusez-moi,*" he said. *C'est une erreur. Une faute. Une mis-compréhension.*"

"*Un malentendu,*" corrected the manager.

Andrew explained as best he could why he and Kelly had left without paying, and he promised to return the following day to pay the bill.

Knowing that the cost of the lunch would cut into his and Kelly's travel money, we offered to pick up the tab. Our offer was accepted with gratitude and apologies. The wine had cost more than the food! They were mortified.

The following day, in mid-afternoon, after the last of the diners had left, the young couple arrived at the restaurant.

The manager was waiting for them.

Having regained his composure, realizing that the delinquent diners were not thieves but simply befuddled American college students and that the whole sorry affair was the result of a misunderstanding, the manager ushered them into a private dining room and invited them to join him at the table. The bill was produced. They added a generous tip and paid in cash.

"*Et maintenant, à l'amitié!*" beamed the manager as a bottle of champagne and a tray of pastries were produced.

All was forgiven. For their part, Kelly and Andrew were chastened by the experience and more than a tad disappointed. When they had believed that their meal had been on the house, they had laughingly christened the famous restaurant "La Tour Sans Argent,"—The Tower Without Money—but now it had reverted to its old identity, La Tour d'Argent (the Silver Tower). The clear blue skies of their idyllic afternoon had definitely clouded over. Fortunately, the clouds had a fittingly silver lining: Andrew and Kelly learned for themselves the hard lesson that "there's no such thing as a free lunch." The lesson might not have had architectural significance, but of all the educational experiences that their grants had enabled, this was undoubtedly the most memorable.

# Captions
## James B. Nicola


Since all my shots could never really show
the subtlety of Scotland's gloaming light,
but only, like a post card, show a sight
or face of some place I would have you go
or meet, I put my camera down to write
and tried to convey what I'd have you know
through prose and poems. And kept doing so
till faced with sights I knew I could not cite:

The sunset after rain. . . A still's rainbow. . .
Loch Druich—oh especially at night,
rippling reflected star flecks. . . .  So in spite
of ardent words I'd started, I took photos after all to show you now, although
the feelings in the faces aren't quite right.

# Druich
## James B. Nicola

Imagine Telluride, the canyon town,
its snow-capped mountains ringing up and down
each side and at the cul-de-sac, with falls
and streams laced up and down the canyon walls.
Then picture it, say, six Tellurides broader:
the middle, not a western town, but water,
and several times the length, a finger bay;
its hand, the sea, not Dolores and Ridgeway.

Feeding it, brooks and rills on every side,
the same as mountain streams in Telluride.
The climate, though, is not dry but too soggy,
which makes the soil, in places, a bit boggy;
instead of sagebrush, heather marls, which bloom
in purples brief as golds of gorse and broom.
Its briefness makes their beauty all the sweet-
er, doomed, in afterlife, to turn to peat.
No street is straight, and everything's unplanned,
organic. . . . That's Loch Druich in Scotland,

where jewels of wildflowers line the side
of any path, like trails in Telluride.
We hiked a *brae* one day, lit on a *broch*,
or ringed stone fort, a mile above the loch;
then kept on, climbing high enough to spy
the Skye Bridge and, beyond, the Isle of Skye.
Returning from Loch Druich to Glasgow
we saw, after a rain, a great rainbow;

later, another, twice as high and wide.

I'd seen a triple one in Telluride
where likewise drivers stopped, poured out of cars;
and others out of homes, schools, stores and bars
all gently understanding, standing under,
as sudden as if we'd been struck by thunder. . . .

Though overseas it wears a foreign face
enchantment is enchantment any place.

# Two Halves of a Whole
## Catherine Dowling

The road to McCarthy, Alaska, runs right up against the Wrangell Mountains. This is bear country, land of ice floes, glaciers, and rivers so swift and cold they take your breath away. Unless you know what you're doing, you can go no further, not without a mountain guide or a small plane. I've come here from Ireland for a week-long writer's workshop sponsored by the Wrangell Mountain Center—writing about nature in the middle of nature. In truth, the workshop is not my top priority. I've really come to experience Alaska away from the tourist trail, and when it comes to out-of-the-way travel, McCarthy doesn't disappoint. It's as near as I'll ever get to the romance of the American frontier.

The little town is about 300 miles east of Anchorage, the last 60 miles a dirt road. It lies within the boundaries of the Wrangell-St. Elias National Park, which the park website says is the size of Yellowstone, Yosemite, and Switzerland combined. Here, out of necessity, power is solar or from generators, rainwater is recycled, and garbage is composted or burned in wood stoves. The non-flush toilet for the electricity-free cabin I'm staying in is in a shack outside, and if I want a shower, it's a bucket hanging over a wooden stall in the back yard of the Center. There is no wasting of water here, no prissy daily grooming or laundering of clothes. I've been here three days, and I can't find my comb, and what's worse, it doesn't matter.

Gardens in McCarthy are higgledy-piggledy affairs vaguely filling the spaces between wood cabins. I sit in a McCarthy garden that struggles to hold its shape against the wildness nibbling at its edges. At the far end of the garden, a row of aspen saplings, young and pliant, rustle in the breeze. Fuchsia-colored fireweed crowds their base, soft contrast to the slatey smoothness of bark. To the right, invisible from where I sit, McCarthy Creek races through the bowl of mountains that surround us. Out past the tenuous boundary of the garden, black bears are known to roam.

"Quirky details. Do you have all the quirky details that bring this scene to life?" the teacher asks. She's a famous writer with a light, tinkly voice that reminds me of silver. I look up from my writing assignment, and a picture of a flush toilet flashes before me. While I never use toilet rim cleaner—those little things that hang over the rim of the bowl and send blue stuff cascading down with every flush—I long for the fragrance of toilet cleaner.

In the afternoon, we move into the old false-fronted village hardware store, now home to the Wrangell Mountain Center. The unpainted log building is roughhewn and weather-battered and looks like it hasn't been upgraded in a hundred years. Another teacher takes over, her voice deeper, more robust. She tackles weighty subjects—wildness and awareness, union and communion, spirit and abandon. Unusual in my experience of the United States, I'm the only non-American in the group. The teacher asks me about Celtic spirituality, much revered in recent times, and about Celtic Warrior Women in particular. I've no idea what she's talking about. "You don't know what a Celtic Warrior Woman is," she says, more a shocked statement than a question, and I'm acutely aware that everyone in the class is looking at me. I stumble over an explanation, embarrassed. "It's your heritage," she tells me. "You should embrace your heritage." I am exceedingly irritated.

———— ✦ ————

After class, I meander through the town heading for the little museum housed in an old railroad depot. There, I find some Irish names, copper miners from the other side of the world who somehow found their way to Kennicott, a tiny copper mining village a few miles from McCarthy. I also find references to Margaret Keenan Harrais, described as an abolitionist, suffragist, and one of the town's first school teachers. She arrived in McCarthy in 1924 when the town had 120 residents—a lot more than it does today. She lobbied hard for a pension scheme for Alaska's teachers and tried to expand the scope of education in McCarthy. Given that McCarthy was then a frontier town well known for its hard-drinking men and hardworking prostitutes, and Margaret was an advocate of the temperate life, could she, I wonder, be described as a Warrior Woman.

I move quickly past displays of empty spice cans, bottles, coffee pots, and old clothes and wonder vaguely how much the rusty mining bucket wedged against a wall weighs. After examining an array of photos sepia with age, I go back outside into the grey, overcast afternoon. The weather reminds me of home. There's a log on the other side of the street where I sit to admire the symmetrical lines of the museum, burgundy and white against the dark green pines beside it. The building is a little smaller than the old three-room school where I began kindergarten, the only school in a rapidly expanding suburb of 1960s Dublin. There we sat at wooden desks with grooves for our pencils and empty ceramic inkwells—we were too young to be let loose with ink. That is where I first heard about the women of ancient and medieval Ireland.

A few names come to mind easily as I rest on the log—Maeve, Grace, Brigid—but the details are elusive. Eventually, scraps of memory fight their way through the fog of decades, history lessons I revisited in high school and again in college. I recall something about how Brigid—Saint Brigid—tricked a bishop into giving her enough land on which to build her monastery, how she may have been made a bishop herself. If that was true, it was quite an achievement. A female triumph over the all-male Catholic Church. But try as I might, I can't remember any teacher or professor using the words Warrior Woman. The summer day is cooling rapidly—not that it was very warm to begin with—so I abandon my mental workout and wander back toward the cabin.

Along the way, I admire the low, shingled buildings, some as weathered and charmingly dilapidated as the hardware store, others freshly painted in vibrant rust red, green, blue, yellow. There's a bar, a take-out restaurant, a backpacker hostel. My favorite is the hotel, a petite two-story building, meticulously cared for, beautifully restored. Flowers spill over the edges of baskets hanging from the porch. In the evening, it glows with light like something out of a cowboy movie, if cowboys had generators, that is. But the space between buildings is wide and scrubby, the streets unpaved. Even the most spruced up structures exude a whiff of wildness, of nature tamed, but only for now.

———— ✦ ————

"Draw a square around a word or a phrase," the teacher with the silver voice is back. "Let it be a window into something else, whatever comes to mind." I square off some words I've just written, then wait. A pearl of water drops onto the page. Earlier, I stuck my head into the outdoor shower to wash my hair but made a poor job of drying it. I rub the water into a streak across the page, stare at the squared-off words, and wonder, can I make it to the end of the week without stepping all the way into the shower and tipping a bucket of cold water onto myself. Then suddenly, the word Maeve comes to mind. I write it down. The teacher is correct, ideas begin to flow, some of the details that eluded me outside the museum yesterday.

Maeve (Irish: Medb) Queen of Connacht may have been a 1st-century historical figure, or she may have been a mythological goddess. Reliable sources from the dark ages are hard to come by, so while members of the jury are still deliberating, they're leaning toward myth. Either way, Maeve was a formidable woman. She reigned over the province of Connacht in the west of Ireland and could summon militia from all over the country to support her when she went to war, as she often did, with her mortal enemy, the king of Ulster (present-day Northern Ireland).

The other name I remembered at the museum was Grace. Grace O'Malley really did exist. She stalked the same Connacht as Maeve, but 1,400 years later, during the reign of Queen Elizabeth 1 of England. Grace came from a wealthy, powerful, seafaring family. As I write, I recall something about how when she was a child, her father refused to take her to sea with him because, he said, her long hair would catch in the ropes of the boat. She promptly cut off her flowing curls, so he had no choice but to take her along. It earned her the nickname Granuaile, *Bald Grace*. It also kick-started her career as a pirate. She went on to ferment and lead rebellions against British rule in Ireland. I run out of steam, put my pen down. Most of my classmates are still writing, so I lean back to enjoy the watery sunshine and air that is as unpolluted as it gets.

After class, I again wander the town's few streets. But this time, in the late evening northern light, I see things I hadn't seen before. Rusted metal wheels and spikes and things I don't recognize pockmark the grass. Behind the facade of a building, rubble and debris, what looks like the entire contents of the house, lie strewn about, no attempt made to clean it up. I'm shocked. I don't know why. I've seen this kind of thing before, on vacant lots in New York City, but here, in the crystal air of a vast wilderness, it's jarring.

As I walk, I think of Maeve and Grace, the Warrior Women I've been told to embrace. For most of my life, I've leaned toward pacifism. Both Maeve and Grace were warriors. The word *warrior* is suffused with romance and righteousness. These women were killers; they thought nothing of leading men, and probably some other women, into battle, thought nothing of starting wars out of pure hubris or jealousy. Maeve murdered her own sister, Eithne, while Eithne was pregnant. At the end of her life, Grace O'Malley changed sides and fought for the British against her fellow countrymen, the men and women she once led into battle. I wonder does my teacher understand that. These are not role models I care to embrace. Even Alaska's high-minded pioneer of education, Margaret Keenan Harrais, engaged in a multitude of petty squabbles with parents and school board members that stymied parts of her legacy.

———— ✦ ————

The workshop I'm taking includes two visits to the Kennicott Glacier. The only thing I know about glaciers is that they're disappearing fast, so I'm excited to set off on our first glacier hike. I'm expecting white; I have prepared for it with a pair of ten-dollar Walmart sunglasses. We hike through the woods, examine the plants, crimson soap berries against forest green leaves, deep purple monks' hoods, a profusion of hairy dryas and, here and there, piles of bear scat, proof that talk of roaming bears is not just a game to frighten the tourists. Half an hour into the hike, the woods give way to undulating hills of rubble. It's a scar, a vast ugliness in the midst of the untouched wilderness. The tailings from the copper mine further up the valley? But then I realize it's not man-made. This is the Kennicott Glacier, the foremost part known as the toe, and it's as far as we go for the day.

———— ✦ ————

Wednesday night in McCarthy's only saloon. Electricity, flush toilets…I don't know what to do with myself. If it had a shower, it could be classified as nirvana. I've gotten to know people who live here all summer long and even some who are residents all year. I've heard them described as closed, but I find them very open people. They're full of stories. At first, it's all about the tourists who foolishly leave food in their tents, the local man who weaves his own fabric and can get wild birds to feed from his hand, the daft pick-up lines men use in the bar. But slowly, in the saloon or late at night in people's woodsheds, McCarthy offers up other, darker stories of loneliness, depression, even abuse.

Time for our second glacier hike. We drive the three miles of bumpy dirt road that leads to Kennicott. The village clutches the side of the mountain. If it weren't already there, it would be difficult to imagine anything could stay anchored to such a sheer slope. Unlike McCarthy, Kennicott was a company town, a place to raise children and go to church. So, although the mine dominates the village, the rust-red and white buildings are neat and symmetrical, and very attractive. The village itself seems planned, ordered, holding its own against the magnificent valley below and the peak that towers above it. We pick up our crampons from a guide shop and begin our descent. As we walk to the trailhead, I peep over the edge of the road. The drop is sheer and littered with rusted machinery and assorted debris from the mine. It cascades down the slope towards the glacier that fills the valley floor. This time, it's not shocking, not even surprising.

At the bottom, we hit more of the gray rubble the glacier churns up in its slow, primordial forward movement. A kind young guide helps me strap crampons to my boots and points out the shiny black smoothness emerging through the grit. Black ice. The ice changes color as we climb. Black becomes gray and then magnificently blindingly white near the top of a mound. This is a different world where everything is uniform and featureless. But as I take the time to look, the contours of this strange landscape take shape. White has infinite shades and textures. Its sheenless solidity is run through with streaks of glittering crystals. Veins of gray slope down to pools of translucent blue. Rivers traverse the glacier, cutting paths into blue ice, and, in the distance, the icefall that fills the entire space between two mountains shimmers and shape-shifts in the afternoon sunlight. This world is indescribably beautiful. I want to get lost in the ribbons of crystal.

Back in Kennicott, at the end of our hike, an impromptu street party forms. Someone brings Scotch, and from somewhere

172

else, vodka and soda appear. The guides play music—guitar and banjo. Just below us, the mine debris continues to rust. Someone has skidded down the slope to collect small pieces. They'll turn it into their idea of art. I am six thousand miles from where I started, on the side of a mountain, on the edge of a wilderness that itself is on the edge of a continent, centuries away from Maeve and Grace and the Celtic Warrior Women. I look up from the would-be art collectors. Straight ahead, the mountains glow orange under a blue and gray sky. In the middle distance, the seam between rubble and ice is a meandering line across the valley floor, growing diffuse as the light fades. As the sun sets, the boundary between ice and rubble disappears. They become what they are; one glacier, of a piece, the toe carving out a whole valley for what comes behind it.

I think again briefly of Maeve and Grace. I'll never be able to embrace their warrior nature, but am I too hasty in dismissing them? Maeve was fearless and didn't waste time feigning modesty about her powers not only to lead an army but to beguile any man she set her sights on. She had five husbands, countless lovers, and, I imagine, it never entered her head that being a woman should hold her back in any way. Grace, too, was fearless and refused to bow to the British monarch when they met in London. Both women were supremely confident, independent, and strode through their world the equal of warriors and kings. Maybe like the glacier, their beauty is inseparable from their ugliness. Maybe that's the nature of things—ugliness and beauty interlaced, each giving power to the other. Maybe I have something to learn from my heritage, even if I can't swallow the whole Warrior Woman package. In the meantime, Kennicott Lodge has a cleaned and perfumed flush toilet we can sneak into if we need it, and someone has produced rice cakes and homemade raspberry jam. The perfect last night in the wilderness.

# Hsi-wei and the Little Straw Sandals

Robert Wexelblatt

The most durable achievements of the Sui Dynasty were the rebuilding of the Great Wall and the construction of the Grand Canal. But the brief Sui reign accomplished more. Emperor Wen's reinstatement of the examination system, his penal, land, and currency reforms, along with his promotion of Buddhism, can be justly said to have laid the foundation for the glories of the Tang Dynasty. To carry out the vast Sui construction projects and fight their many wars, thousands were conscripted and countless lives sacrificed. The high taxes were paid in labor or military service. It is not surprising that these losses figure in many of the poems of Chen Hsi-wei, the peasant/poet who spent his life traveling throughout the empire, leaving behind him straw sandals and poems. Hsi-wei lived to see the fall of the Sui Dynasty and the start of its successor. A minister of the new regime, Fang Xuan-ling, an admirer of Hsi-wei's verses, paid a visit to the poet in his retirement and kept a record of their conversations. Fang questioned Hsi-wei about the origins of many poems, including the one people called "The Little Straw Sandals."

———— ✦ ————

As a special gift, Fang Xuan-ling had brought three cakes of green tea, which, he said, was becoming popular at court. After Hsi-wei brewed a pot, they settled down to drink and talk in the tiny cobbled patio Hsi-wei called his courtyard.

Hsi-wei, always courteous, complimented the tea. Fang asked if Hsi-wei recalled a poem popularly known as "The Little Straw Sandals."

The poet put down his cup. "I remember it. It's one where

I tried to say something by not saying it."

"Saying and not saying. Something you picked up from the Chan Buddhists?" Laying his cup aside, Fang reached for his brush, prepared to make a note as he sententiously recited the well-known Chan principle, "Never tell too plainly."

Hsi-wei chuckled. "Oh, nothing so spiritual as that, My Lord."

"Well then, can you tell me how you came to write that poem?"

"I can. In fact, I remember it very well. And who knows? Perhaps if I tell you, you'll see what I wasn't saying."

"As you say, who knows?" Fang finished his tea. "Please proceed, Master Hsi-wei."

"Very well. That summer, I was making my way through Liangzhou when I came to a little village called Yanshi Kun. The place was in a pitiable state, like so many others I saw that year. No dogs barked when I came down the road. All the peasants' hovels were in states of disrepair; the fields were choked with weeds; skinny, half-dressed children ran around or slumped under trees looking exhausted and despondent."

"What was the matter?"

"Yanshi Kun was a village populated by those too old to do much work and those too young to do any at all. The whole district was poor, but Yanshi Kun was destitute."

"Ah, that explains the lack of dogs. They couldn't even afford to feed them."

"My Lord, I'm afraid it was rather the other way around."

Fang, a city man who had always been well off, blushed. "Ah. I didn't think of that."

Hsi-wei, embarrassed to have embarrassed his guest, continued. "Though it wasn't likely I'd find customers, I set up my sign by the village well. People gathered around, not to order sandals but to beg for news. Of course, I couldn't tell them what they really wanted to know—about those who'd gone away. I shared with them what I could, things I'd picked up along the way, but not everything. I didn't tell them about the many deaths at the Canal or the latest reverse in Goguryeo. Things for these people were bad enough as they were."

Fang tried to brighten the mood. "Did you sell any sandals?"

Hsi-wei grinned. "My Lord, you know I did. One pair."

"Then I suppose you had little to do in the village."

"Oh, I was very busy in Yanshi Kun. I made myself useful. I remember fixing a leaking roof and replacing rotted boards on a shed. Though it was late in the season, I even planted some rice for an ancient farmer who couldn't bend over anymore. He kept nodding and smiling at me. I remember tearing weeds from an old woman's vegetable plot. Also, I entertained the children."

"Did you gather them up, or did children just come to you?"

"Some of them had never seen anybody my age, and others must have had happy memories of their parents. It's no wonder they flocked around me. It certainly wasn't due to any merit in me."

"And how did you entertain them?"

"I recited a poem I thought might divert them. It's about a smart little girl named Mai Ling. I don't suppose you know it?"

Fang made a serious face, concentrating. "I think I might. Do you have a copy?"

"I do. Would you like to read it?"

"I'd like it even better if you read it to me."

The poet rose and went into his two-room cottage and returned with a small, not very clean scroll.

Saying "As you wish, My Lord," Hsi-wei unfurled the scroll and read the poem people call "Mai Ling's Good Idea."

*Long ago, there was war between Night and Day.*
*They taunted and insulted one another, all spite and spleen.*
*Like a woolen blanket, Night tried to blot out Day*
*while Day, like a bonfire, toiled to outshine the stars.*
*From these mighty battles, people and animals suffered,*
*enjoying respites only at noontime and midnight.*

*With Winter and Summer, it was much the same.*
*They detested each other and all the more*
*for being so evenly matched. Midsummer and Midwinter*
*were calm, but, in between, the seasons' wrestled ceaselessly;*
*raising tempests and earthquakes to afflict the world.*

*One day, as her grandparents were complaining of it all,*
*Mai Ling spoke up, a little girl of just eight years.*
*"Nobody can tell me what time is or how much there is of it.*
*So, why not just make more? Then Uncle Winter can have*
*his time and Auntie Summer hers; then Day can be day*
*all day and Night can be night the whole night through."*

*Mai Ling's grandfather laughed indulgently, as old men do.*
*But her granny reproached him. "Listen to the child.*
*New eyes see better than old ones." And so the people*
*convened a parley with Day and Night, and invited*
*Winter and Summer too. When all were settled,*
*Day and Night and Winter and Summer glaring*
*At one another, Mai ling got up explained her idea.*

*"Uncle Day, when you get sleepy, you shouldn't struggle.*
*Auntie Night, when you're worn out, you ought to go to bed.*
*You shouldn't rub your eyes and spite each other.*
*Neighbors need boundaries, little walls, not too high.*
*We can make new time if only you'll agree.*
*We'll set fences between you: Dusk and Dawn.*

*"And as for you, Uncle Winter and Auntie Summer,*
*you should do the same and not crash into each other*
*ruining our rice with untimely heat and blasts of cold.*
*Let's set new seasons between you, just little ones, low walls.*
*As Winter tires, we'll have Spring, and as Summer fades, Fall.*

*That's my idea. In the night, people and animals can go*

*to sleep and during the day we'll work and play.*
*In Spring, we'll sow, and in the Fall, we'll harvest.*
*Then you can stop this nasty wrangling and enjoy yourselves.*
*Then we shall all be grateful to you, blessing*
*Each day and every night, each season and every year."*

"I'd forgotten how charming it was," said Fang, smiling at the picture of happy youngsters in his head. "The children must have been delighted."

Hsi-wei didn't reply at once and, when he did, it was in a somber tone. "My Lord, the village was very poor; the children were terribly hungry."

"I can imagine."

"With respect, I'm not sure you can. Those children didn't have enough strength to express delight. But they did sit quietly, so I was able to give their grandparents a little time to themselves. And the people were generous with me, as the poor usually are. The less they have, the more they share. The old couple whose thatch I repaired wanted to give me their bed, though it was only a burlap rice sack stuffed with rushes. 'We'll sleep on the floor beside the children. It will be a pleasure for us.' I declined, of course, and took myself to the shed I'd repaired. The pigs were long gone.

"The next day, I did some more work, mostly lifting things, as I recall. An old woman watched me, impossible to say whether with approval or suspicion. A tiny, barefoot toddler was clinging to her. He kept saying 'Zumu, Zumu,' as he tugged at her skirt. It sounded like a whine, a plea. He was as thin as the others, but his stomach was swollen."

"Ah, a big stomach? Then he was well fed?"

Hsi-wei shook his head, again embarrassed to have to explain. "No, My Lord. It's what happens to children who are starving."

Fang had nothing to say to that, and Hsi-wei quickly resumed.

"In the afternoon, it grew hot. The old woman led the boy

over to a dusty willow tree and sat him down with a group of children lolling in the shade."

"The old woman in the poem?"

"Yes. Mrs. Chu. Another old woman told me later that Mrs. Chu's son had been lost in Goguryeo and, to pay the tax, her daughter-in-law went to the Canal. That was the year before, when the boy was barely two years old. No one expected his mother to come back except Mrs. Chu. Though the boy was falling asleep, I could hear him still murmuring 'Zumu,' but quietly now, with resignation. That was when she approached me.

"'You make sandals?' she asked. I said I did.

"She nodded toward the willow. 'My grandson is walking now. His mother will be so surprised. I've been thinking. I want to buy him a pair of sandals. How much would that cost?'

Hsi-wei stopped, and the two men were quiet.

"Another cup of tea?" Hsi-wei offered.

"I know what you were telling without telling," said Fang. "Yes?"

"The verses are present, also Mrs. Chu, the boy, and the sandals. I remember you also said something interesting about your feelings concerning your work. But the poem's really about what's missing, isn't it? About who's missing. The dogs, the pigs, but most of all the parents."

Hsi-wei smiled, got to his feet, collected their cups, and went to fetch more green tea.

———— ✦ ————

## THE LITTLE STRAW SANDALS

*Mrs. Chu ordered sandals for her grandson*
*Wanglei. She beamed, proud that the boy could*
*Already walk. "They'll be his first," she said.*
*She took something from the pocket of her skirt.*
*It was a little Wanglei-sole-sized cucumber.*
*"This is how small you're to make them."*

*Fashioning such tiny sandals isn't simple.*
*I used the finest straw, pulled the strands*
*Taut, made the knots tight, and carefully sliced*
*off the loose ends. I made them sturdy too.*
*Wanglei was bound to be rough on them.*
*Straw sandals are humble, useful, honest,*
*Like Mrs. Chu, who tried to pay me.*

*I've had more customers than readers.*
*I like when people admire their new sandals,*
*Hold them up, turn them this way and that,*
*And say it must have been hard to make them.*
*But I'm even happier when they say that*
*Making straw sandals must be easy for me.*
*To tell the truth, it's no different with my poems.*

# A Conversation with Abby Frucht

*Lowestoft Chronicle*

Abby Frucht
(Photography: Abby Frucht)

Winner of the prestigious Iowa Short Fiction Award in 1987 for her first collection of stories, *Fruit of the Month*, which published the next year, Abby Frucht followed this prize with a highly acclaimed first novel, *Snap*, which went on to become a *New York Times* Notable Book of the Year. Two of her subsequent four novels were also *New York Times* Notable Books. Her story collection *The Bell at the End of a Rope*, published in 2012, was her first book in over twelve years and her first collection of stories in twenty-five years.

In this exclusive interview with *Lowestoft Chronicle*, Abby Frucht discusses her novels and story collections and her distinguished writing career.

**Lowestoft Chronicle (LC):** I've heard you say you were drawn to writing from a very young age and that you had filled a lot of little notebooks with poems and drawings by the time you were nine years old. When did your interests turn to fiction? Are there any particular writers you remember as having influenced your writing during those childhood years?

**Abby Frucht (AF):** My favorite book when I was just starting to read on my own was Louis Untermeyer's *The Golden Treasury of Poetry*, which included many narrative poems like "The Highwayman" and "The Owl and the PussyCat," so my interest in stories was stoked in part by poetry, and indeed, most of my own first poems told stories (and some of the stories I write today might be mistaken for poems.) As for fiction itself, I must have read *Chitty Chitty Bang Bang* (the original Ian Fleming version, which I loved for its irreverence and for its comical drawings) two hundred times. Fleming didn't talk down to children at all; in fact, he made reading his whimsical and darkly magical story (which featured a female child every bit the intellectual equal of the book's scary but hilarious crop of villains) feel like a conspiratorial act.

**LC:** When did you actively start writing for publication? *Ontario Review, Agni Review, Epoch,* and *Indiana Review* were some of your early writing credits, but what was the first story you had published? Were you sending out a lot of pieces to literary magazines when you graduated from university?

**AF:** I never received a higher degree. Instead, on graduating college with a major in English and a minor in Biology, I worked in a variety of ice cream parlors and sandwich shops in St. Louis, during which time I started reading contemporary fiction writers and sending out my own stories. My worst rejection of all came from my parents when I was visiting home and showed them the first thirty or so pages of my first novel in progress. They had encouraged my writing all my life and went on to be proud readers of mine, but when my dad read those awful, awful (and they were really awful!) pages, his response was, "Nothing happens, Hon," and my mom said, maybe since we had just gone whale watching that day, "Would you like to become a marine biologist?"

**LC:** Your story collection, *Fruit of the Month*, the co-winner of the Iowa Short Fiction Award, also garnered praise from *The New York Times*, *Publishers Weekly*, and the *Los Angeles Times* when it was published. What made you decide to submit it to the Iowa Short Fiction Award competition?

**AF:** I was young, and I didn't have an agent yet, and that was simply the first thing that occurred to me. I remember getting a phone call one night from one of the contest readers there telling me how much he liked it and that he hoped it would go on to win. The reader, a grad student, was Pinckney Benedict. We became good friends as the years went on, and his marvelous collection of stories, *Town Smokes*, is one that I assign to this day to my students. I have never had a student who didn't love it.

**LC:** When it comes to beginning a story, I've heard you say you start with a voice that moves you, and the story arises out of the process of writing or out of the language. Do you outline at all, Abby?

**AF:** I never outline. I write very much on the sentence level. I try to reside inside of each sentence and explore all of its possibilities in order to see what it has to teach me about voice, character, and story. If it doesn't teach me enough, I go out of my way to feed more possibilities into it, like clues, to see where they might lead me, and if they lead me nowhere, then I abandon that sentence and maybe, eventually or at once, that story. I do it this way not because I advocate for it being the best way to write a story but because I enjoy that process. It might sound like a soulless process, but really the soul of the story, for me anyway, is to be found in the vocabulary, the punctuation, the syntax, the arrangement of idea, observation, event, remark, and finally, in whatever intervenes, either from the inside or from the outside, with those first four things.

**LC:** With regard to your first novel, *Snap*, you've said that your motivation for writing it was a desire to learn how to write a novel. How would you describe the experience of writing that book? And was writing *Snap* a long process? I know your books go through many redrafts, but *Snap* was published even before *Fruit of the Month* came out.

**AF:** At the time I wrote *Snap*, I had a new baby, my first, so it's almost impossible to divide the experience of writing that book from being a new parent. Disregarding those first thirty pages, which I threw away at once and started writing again entirely from scratch, writing *Snap* never felt arduous or impossible. I never felt blocked, and being a new mother, my ego was entirely uninvolved. I simply followed my instincts, and I hardly so much as questioned my writing impulses. Since I was living for several months in Australia, where my husband at the time was doing research there, part of *Snap* was written by hand (at home, I used an IBM Selectric) in a metal hut in the middle of a bird sanctuary filled with flies, wombats, and koalas, which make a sound like a motorcycle, and part of it was written in a balcony in Manly, a suburb of Sidney where people held dog shows and dance recitals amid flocks of hungry seagulls on a seaside promenade. Never did it feel like a long time, to me. The days were full and bizarrely unfamiliar, and they passed. I did have an agent for *Snap*, which came out so close to when *Fruit of the Month* was published that the two books were reviewed as a pair, first in the *New York Times Book Review* and then in a number of other places. Many of those book review pages no longer exist, and nor does *Snap*'s publisher, Ticknor & Fields, which was part of the original Houghton Mifflin, which now publishes in the field of education. The only thing that's still the same is the University of Iowa Press, and they should be congratulated for it.

**LC:** Many of the major US periodicals have reviewed your fiction, from *Newsday* and *The New Yorker* to *The New York Times*. How important was that book review by Charles

Dickinson in *The New York Times*? He writes highly of both books, and for a debut author, that must be incredibly rewarding, as well as very advantageous to a writer's career.

**AF:** Yes, that kind of early attention was incredibly important, though I had no idea, then, what a big deal it was since, as I've said, I was ignorant (and still am, actually), fairly happy to be ignorant of such things. Although I am forever and eternally grateful to have a life as a writer and a reader, I'm simply not the kind of person who craves fame or big success, which is a good thing since I don't have it. But back to the *New York Times*; I might never have been welcomed as faculty at Vermont College of Fine Arts, for instance, without that early attention, especially since I have no higher degree, and nor might many of the other aspects of my professional trajectory (my life as a reviewer and an essayist and as the recipient of grants, and yes, as a novelist) have occurred in precisely the way that they did.

**LC:** You've written for *The Boston Globe*, *The Philadelphia Inquirer*, *The Village Voice*, *Chicago Tribune*, and *The New York Times*. How did you get involved in journalism, Abby?

**AF:** I began by writing book reviews when I published my first novels, and from there, I began writing longer literary essays and then personal essays. Writers who wish to write book reviews would be well advised to look into joining The National Book Critics Circle, by the way, which provides a freelance guide as well as many other resources.

**LC:** How did your second novel, *Licorice*, come to be published through the prestigious independent non-profit publisher Graywolf Press? Did the publisher approach you, or did they seem like a great fit for the book?

**AF:** If I remember correctly, Katrina Kenison, *Snap*'s editor, had retired from her work at Ticknor & Fields by then (she went on to edit the Best American Series, I think, and is also a writer). It was my agent's idea to send the book to Graywolf. I don't think that I, myself, had even heard of Graywolf before he told me that my book had been accepted there, but they really did end up being the perfect fit for the book. I loved my entire experience with Graywolf—their cover for *Licorice* is by far my favorite of all my book's covers, not including the tweedy looking milkmaid lounging across the cover of the Croatian edition of *Are You Mine?*, and the publicity they did for me was ultimately more meaningful than that of any of the bigger presses who published me later on. I remember, once, phoning my publicist at one of those big New York houses when one of my novels was just coming out, and my own publicist didn't know who I was!

**LC:** You said of your fifth novel, *Polly's Ghost*, that you "wanted the book to mirror more the chaos of real life than the neat preconceived frame of my other novels." As all of your previous novels were critically successful books, did you have any concerns about the change of direction?

**AF:** No. I just wanted to do something different than what I had done before. *Polly's Ghost* received a mixed reception; some people thought it was too digressive, and other people called it a "triumph." Personally, I like the sort of random reach it exercised, and if it's a triumph for me, that's part of the reason why.

**LC:** *The Bell at the End of a Rope* contains fourteen stories connected somewhat to childhood, written over a period of nearly twenty years. "My childhood neighborhood and many of my childhood friends, neighbors, babysitters, family members and pastimes were included." Your story, "Bride," isn't included, although it seems like it might fit in the collection. What made you decide on these particular stories, and as there is no title story in this collection, what made you choose this title for the book?

**AF:** When I put the book together, I was toying with the idea of someday writing a novel in which "Bride" would be a part, so I decided that it would be a mistake to include it in the collection. I haven't ended up writing that novel, so now that you mention it, I wish I had included "Bride"!

As for my reason for including the stories I did include, I wanted the book to represent a range of styles and approaches to story writing since each story really *IS* an experiment, to me. For some reason, when I write stories, my inclination is not to write a story like one I've written before. This collection demonstrates that impulse.

The title comes from the first paragraph of the story "Is Glistening," which reads:

*Throughout the house, but mainly in the kitchen, were all sorts of objects from Mexico. The painted chair, the saltshaker in the shape of a bird, the platter, an apron, the tablecloth. The blanket, the Oaxacan bowl, the papier mache skeleton, the bell at the end of a rope.*

The reason I chose that last phrase for the title is that I thought it sounded childlike and because it provided me an image of a child's hand reaching for the rope but not being quite able to reach it, and so not being able to ring it without help. The stories are the help.

**LC:** Although published in 2000, you completed *Polly's Ghost* in 1999. Have you been working on a novel since that book, Abby, or have you been concentrating solely on short stories?

**AF:** Since that time, I wrote one novel that didn't work, and then, in addition to the stories, I've become very fond of essay writing. When I wrote the stories in *The Bell at the End of a Rope*, mainly what I wanted was to celebrate people's inner lives, particularly the inner lives of children and of parents as they relate to their children. I'm now collaborating on a novel with my friend and VCFA [Vermont College of Fine Arts] colleague, Laurie Alberts. We're having a huge amount of fun with it since it's a different kind of project for both of us.

Too, life is complicated, in bad ways and in good ways. Most of the complications in my life over the last decade have been in good ways, or maybe it would be more accurate to say that even the bad ways have evolved, somehow, into good ways. I think that's the best answer that I can bring at this time to that question, which I thank you for asking.

# Woman with the Red Carry-On
## Jacqueline Jules

She wheels a red carry-on
hardly higher than her knee,
not much wider than her waist
as I watch with wonder,
wishing I could do that,
could take essentials only.
Leave behind the extra black dress
packed in case I feel fat
in the print I planned to wear.

Why must I take six undies
for a two night stay? A spare
blouse in case I spill my coffee?
A second pair of shoes,
in case a heel breaks?

Why can't I be that woman
with the red carry-on?
Stepping through the airport
back straight, chin up
confident I have
everything I need
to face the world
away from home.

# My Happy Place
Jacqueline Jules

"Hand on your heart," she says.
"Visualize your happy place."

"It's a cruise ship," I answer.
"The one I took six months after."

"Breathe," she reminds.

Salt air cleanses my lungs.

I'm standing on the stern,
watching the water foam
in thick white trails.

At the back of the boat,
no one is judging me,
wondering if my grief
lingers too long.

I can throw tears over the rail
like ashes. I can rock inside
the sound of swirling water.

I can whisper into the waves.

And I can feel him near me,
listening.

# No Entiendo
## Robert Mangeot

*Serpientes.* Rafael, the resort guy, said, "*las serpientes.*" I knew
zero Spanish besides greetings and single-digit numbers, but
serpent was a word that slithered past language barriers. It took
on amped menace out in the dark forest and thunder. I hoped
against hope Rafael had stopped us on the drenched trail to
stress his careful lengths devised to avoid snakes entirely. I was
here at Punta Papagayo installing a hospitality-grade printing
and scanning solution with in-room network capabilities. No
way, no how did I sign on for *serpiente*-by-night Costa Rica.

Rafael grinned and waggled his arm like a sidewinder
coming in hot. My chest caught as if the poncho added a
sudden hundred pounds.

"You copy, Front Desk?" I said into the walkie. "There's a
snake situation."

Static fizzled off the radio. "Beck!" came Marta, the resort
liaison, voice broken in spurts. "How is your hike?"

"Repeat: imminent serpent encounter."

"It is nothing. Enjoy your walk."

No right mind labeled sidewinders as nothing. This
cove eco-resort teemed with a great many beaked, clawed,
and fanged man-killers. And I had fangs inbound. Amid a
monsoon. I deserved a hazard bonus and cover story in every
printer-copier trade journal going.

Rafael swept his flashlight where our muddy excuse for a
path wound past monster trees tangled with vines like a snake
god itself designed the forest. At the hilltop, the highest point
from beachside stood the satellite dish at its reinforced shack.
No, I had not trekked up there yet. Yes, this was Wednesday,
and the easy-install timetable guarantee had ended on Monday.
The resort manager vowed beet-faced to drop-kick me out into

this very serpent den tonight unless he printed high-res color menus. It wasn't my fault his business plan hinged on sketchy wi-fi and phone cable strung down from Snake Central.

It was Punta Papagayo's laminated nature handbook that'd gotten me. It flapped open as twelve folds front and back, seven folds dedicated wholly to snakes: bushmaster, fer-de-lance, coachwhip, burrowing python, jumping pit viper. A handbook suspiciously unavailable on their website for advance reading.

I fell in behind Rafael grudgingly. Here was what I knew about him: not a frigging iota. He'd materialized at my elbow after Marta presented the shack key. Rafael might've been a credentialed naturalist, or he might've been a second shift bartender, or he might've been the insane operative of a hillside snake cult. He'd brought no rifle or machete, no first aid. He wore a resort golf shirt and khakis and looked set to greet any arriving boa or cougar. Punta Papagayo had big cats, Marta happened to mention only after I'd signed their liability waiver.

Marta. As soon as the Liberia shuttle dropped me off car sick from backroad ruts, Marta thrust at me a guaro sour, which I discovered was sugar and lighter fluid. She'd brought my room service meals herself, plantains and conch ceviche, and this beans and rice breakfast called rooster. She'd tried teaching me the marimbas and introducing me to the resident macaws. Basically, those were jackass parrots. The red one that dangled upside down from the lobby gutter and didn't respect me a lick was named Duende. No clue what it meant. I might've asked Marta if she wanted to get a beer or something, but women like her would've had boyfriends with better jobs than copier guy, plus Duende always hung there ready to snip me open.

"*Escorpiones*," Rafael said horror movie sharp. For unnecessary effect, he flicked his index finger like a striking tail.

"What about scorpions?" I said. Rafael grinned his serial killer grin, so I asked that same question of Marta on the walkie. "You're obligated to explain."

"Relax," Marta said, almost lost in crackle. "The animals are not much out in the storms."

"About that. You said the heavy stuff rumbled some ways off over some mountains."

"Yes. It arrives from the *cordillera* soon. Hurry with your work, please."

Rafael turned his other arm into a mock snake that sprung on the unsuspecting scorpion finger. "Seriously," I said, and here I was pressing the talk button pretty hard. "Tell this dude we're scrubbing this mission. Tell him I no *hablo*."

"Say *no entiendo*," Marta said. "'I do not understand.'"

"Do you get much cult activity here?"

"This is good for you, Beck. Tonight, you experience Guanacaste."

Lightning flashed the trail into 3-D shadows. I understood Punta Papagayo enough. I understood I'd been lured to a coastal reptile park fretting each next moment could anger a viper with mad vertical leap. Afternoons, I would venture out to network the bungalow wall tablets, dozens of bungalows engulfed by tropical snake habitat. Other than that, I kept myself shut in my room where at least I had a solid defensive position unless that raccoon picked the window locks. Night by night, it seemed to be making headway on the lever mechanisms.

It mystified me what jazzed people over soaking dire experiences out of life. It was like when I'd quit Wiffle ball. I'd owned my brothers at Wiffle ball until I found that mammoth corn snake sunning itself on home plate. It'd swallowed a rodent of some kind. Mom tried swearing that corn snakes meant a vibrant backyard, to which I said she could go cut the grass then. Mom took me to pet stores and zoos so I could acclimate to reptiles, but forcible snake-viewing turbo-charged my desire for an indoors technical career with survival not in regular doubt.

For a while, Rafael strode on at his clip, me wobbling after him. Somehow, I broke an all-over sweat in driving rain. Best I could decipher, Rafael was pointing out the various plants and their tropical leaves fit for smothering a guy and something that, based on how he wriggled his arm again, was truly horrible there lurking in the branches. Rafael grinned on while Marta was all chuckles over the walkie.

"What?" I said. "What's so funny?"

"You would have to know Rafa," Marta said.

"Was it about snakes?"

"*Arbóreo*," Rafael said.

"Hang on," I told him. "I'm getting you translated."

"*Pura vida.*"

Lightning zipped across the clouds. The radio dissolved into perma-static. Great. Now it was Rafael and me, and he was tapping a sneaker at downed palm fronds. "*Aquí tambien*," Rafael said. With that, he tromped up the path. I jabbed at the radio's talk button while I stumbled after him. This was how I would go out, then. Bit and constricted to death over Punta Papagayo's under-investment in satellite broadband.

Rafael stopped and shone his flashlight on a leaf bigger than the steering wheel of an ATV I should've been escaping in. Squatting in his beam lay a neon green frog, its eyes a brimstone red.

"*Muy rara*," Rafael said.

My heart threatened to break through my ribs. I would've expected amphibians oozed a stepped-down menace from major reptiles, but this thing glistened with dangerous and deadly skin, and it seared me with radioactive eyes.

Rafael photographed his devil frog at multiple zooms and angles like it was nature's own miracle. With him distracted, I could double back, text Marta my resignation, and hammer in-room beers until the morning shuttle rode me bone-jarred to Liberia Airport. I might've done that, except these were gale-force conditions, and downhill was super dark, and shapes moved through the forest. New plan. I could root myself nice and quiet on this path, pray that red-eyed frogs didn't crave flesh and the rain kept apex predators somewhere dry. It was ten or eleven hours to first light. I'd gone to the bathroom before we left. I could do this.

That frog blinked at me. Blinked. At me. Kept staring. My road to sweet bunker safety meant fixing whatever mess waited in the receiver shack.

I motioned Rafael to get us going. He was gone up the trail with speed and a grin. Sure, he might well spring a net or pit trap, but I'd stopped blaming him for anything. Cultists did what they did. This was all on Marta and her persistent encouragement about life experiences. Her never-you-mind over a seven-fold horde of snakes. I dismissed her masterminding a plausibly deniable murder-slash-human sacrifice only because whacking the copier guy didn't make sense before their print-and-copy solution was fully installed.

Further up the hillside, the trail narrowed to where Punta Papagayo was a constant scratch and scrabble at my arms and legs. I followed Rafael across a run-off stream—Costa Rica had water moccasins, per the handbook—and plunged through nettles and thorns and who knew what poison leaves. Headway. I'd made actual headway before lack of oxygen bent me over.

Troops of ants carted leaf bits off for nowhere humans ought to follow along the ground and branches. Probably they had a species name like shrieking bloodbath ants. The immediate question was how debilitating their bite, and I could've guessed that answer.

It was strange what a person mulled through in forest primeval with himself and a billion ants and a demon frog around. For one, how those ants didn't swarm me. Those ants farmed their frigging ant hearts out, leaf scraps on their backs. Second, I'd been in Guanacaste for days without a snake sighting. Not an airborne pit viper going for the jugular, not even a shoestring spot-belly or snail-eater. Possibly, the Punto Papagayans had developed mutual boundaries with the wildlife except for creeper macaws.

Third, and this might've been an onset of dengue fever, I had a life experience right here in the sideways rain. I was, if not communing with these ants, at some level communing near them, without need of medical triage.

I edged around the farmer ants and maneuvered uphill. Look at me, I thought as I picked safe footholds in the slope. Every meter scaled burned my calves, rang through my body. Soon, my brain set the climb to marimba accompaniment. I plowed onward, rain-pelted and branch-thwacked. I would slap my torn poncho on the property manager's desk and connect him to printing and copying so high-resolution it earned me the presidential suite with unlimited beer and tamper-proof windows.

I broke into a hilltop clearing hacked from the forest. The aluminum receiver shed wavered on a concrete slab that someone must've laid before wi-fi was invented. Steel wires held the satellite dish from getting swooped off by storm gusts. Grass as tall as my soaked frame surrounded a dirt channel across the clearing. A stalking ground, but I crept ahead at a slower marimba beat and reached the shack neither pounced on nor constricted.

Rafael was there and gestured me over toward another apparent degree-of-difficulty caught in his flashlight beam. On closer approach, a hairy mass of spider, its front legs reared for action like a mini martial artist.

"*Tarántula*," Rafael said.

Tarantulas. This was officially a true butt-kicking level of copier installation. If I pulled this off, I might score myself a reality TV adventurer gig. Producers would drop me semi-equipped in Patagonia or the Mojave or Arctic tundra, and I would have to battle raw nature and cobble together makeshift printer-copier solutions.

I undid the shack's padlock and peered in for a light switch. There wasn't one. Horror movies, there never was.

"*Cuidado*," Rafael said.

"Exactly," I said, "if that means extreme IT. I can get you in on a TV deal, maybe."

"*Cuidado. Por favor.*"

I eased my head into the shack. This was it, either next-level overcoming of raw nature or a cultist temple. Inside, I made out a glow off a satellite receiver box and the bulky frames of old-school relay cabinets. Beyond that, the shack corners loomed darker than dark. I shuffled deeper in among junk equipment and circuit board clutter. Above the satellite box table, somebody had strung a bulb on a wire. I fumbled it on, and bam, lumped beside the receiver cabinet, lay a diamond-backed rattlesnake of significant heft.

I froze in my tracks. Adios, marimbas. Hola, serpent maracas. We stayed like that for a near eternity, the snake and I, rain pounding the sheet metal.

"Hello, friend," I squeezed out.

By sound and appearances, the snake didn't feel too friendly. A childhood rewind like you always heard descended upon doomed souls descended on me. Forcible zoo exhibits and my brothers forever sneaking plastic snakes into my bedsheets and lunch bags. Making me watch horror movies where, in death's irony, a poor fool repairman always met his end right at the busted equipment.

"Friend," I said over a whoosh in my ears. "This is weird, I know. But I kind of need to get components installed."

The diamondback coiled itself round and round, clearly willing to re-set my timetable.

"*Cuidado*," I heard someone say from behind. Then a camera shutter rapid-fire as my pulse. Rafael, and too late, I could gauge what *cuidado* meant.

I said, "How about I step off some?" I started to do that, but the snake jacked its hiss factor plenty. "What?" I said. "What, then?"

The snake flared its scaly nostrils. In my impending death fugue, I was running the Wiffle ball bases under a red sun, a raccoon latched onto my leg, Duende, the macaw, perched squawking on my shoulder, and Mom shouting how she was proud my ant-farmed corpse would sustain critical forest. Marta stood at third, hands raised for me to stop. I high-fived her as I staggered around for home. The rattlesnake blocked the plate in strike pose. I heard Marta call, "Beck, you miss the signal." Either she'd spoken life's essential meaning, or else it was my parting break with reality.

Signals. Fugue Marta had nailed it. Punta Papagayo sent constant signals. Damned if I'd fathomed one yet.

"*No entiendo*," I said.

The snake flicked its tongue. Paused its rattle a second.

I risked shrugging an apology. With a final head flourish, the diamondback twisted down the table leg and swept its long, extended self out past Rafael and into the underbrush. Rafael kept photographing the whole time like this was just another Wednesday at Punta Papagayo.

My fugue lingered on awhile. It must've because I heard myself cackling like Duende. Eventually, wracking chills came on, and I smelled musk and rain. Rafael was setting my tools while the wind roiled the shack. Hell, this was just another Wednesday at Punta Papagayo. Just a Wednesday night and the rattlesnake also felt I would benefit from more life experience. Hard to argue. I hadn't even mastered the swim-up bar. Whenever I saw Marta later, raw nature permitting, after her strongest guaro sour, I would print her my man-serpent dialogue photos and brag how I'd even used some Spanish.

# Truck Stop
## Rob Dinsmoor

I'd had a shitload too much coffee, that was the problem. I'd
been driving pretty much nonstop, but I'd stopped for a large
black coffee at a Dunkin' Donuts outside Santa Fe. I was on
schedule to deliver my load to a warehouse in Albuquerque,
but then my guts started to seize up. I figured I'd have about
ten minutes before I'd have to pull to the side of the road and
drop my britches, but Hallelujah, I saw the green and red lights
in the distance. I thought it might be a convenience store, and
as I approached, lo and behold, it was.

The parking lot was empty, which was not surprising seeing
as how it was three in the morning. It was summer, but the
temperature was down to the low sixties now and dropping
like a rock. Even with the light coming from the convenience
store, you could see thousands of stars in the desert night.

I stepped up to the counter, where a tall, skinny kid about
twenty-five years old with a goatee and red, watery eyes was
trying to stay awake. He grinned. "Did you see the big meteor?"

"No," I said impatiently.

"I was outside, having a smoke, and I saw it—it was purple
and looked like it landed not too far away."

I wondered what he'd been smoking, seeing the purple
meteors and all, but then again, if there'd been a meteor, I
probably would've missed it, since my bleary eyes had been
glued to the road.

"Could I get a pack of Marlboros?" I asked. "And while
you're lookin', you got a restroom?"

"Yeah."

"Could I use it?"

"Yeah."

The boy was a little slow on the uptake, confirming my

suspicion he'd been smoking something other than tobacco and it was more than tiredness that was making his eyes red.

"Where is it?"

"Out back. But it's locked."

"Could you give me the—" I started to ask and then stopped and said, "Give me the keys—will you?"

"Out back," he said, and handed me a set of keys mounted on a wooden stick shaped like a cactus. "Just take a right outside the door, then another right."

"Thanks."

I unlocked the men's room and found it to be pretty standard—two toilet stalls right next to each other, a urinal, and a sink. I went into the rear stall and closed the door. I hung my jacket on the little hook on the door. As I was dropping my britches, I pulled my snub-nosed .38 out of the back of my pants and tucked it into the pocket of my jacket. Rather than have it fall in the bowl and get water-logged, which happens more often than you might think.

After a minute or two, I heard the door open—slam open, really, and bang against the wall. Truth be told, it kind of gave me a start. The door to my stall rattled hard, and I said, "This one's taken, buddy. Try the other one."

And then the other door flew open so hard I thought it would pull both stalls over. Then there was a grunt, a heavy torso plopping down, and the splashing of water. No, not splashing, really. Lapping. Like a dog drinking out of the toilet. What the hell?

I was very tempted to say something but figured any guy drinking out of the toilet probably couldn't be reasoned with. I was glad I was packing. It just goes to show, you should always carry a gun, even when you go to the bathroom. I took the pistol out of the pocket of my jacket and undid the safety.

The toilet paper roll on the other side of the wall started spinning. And spinning. And spinning—kind of like a rat in one of those exercise wheels—till I could see a whole pile of it on the floor. I've seen guys do that before and never understood it. Why do you need that much toilet paper? Are you trying to plug up a hole, or just fuck up the plumbing? Another groan, or a sound like a wounded animal, and the whole pile of toilet paper was taken up.

"Jesus! Are you okay over there, buddy?" I asked, almost afraid to deal with this guy at all. There was no answer but a grunt and a snort.

Then the next stall's door swung open and slammed shut. Then I heard the rattle of the paper towel dispenser, and then the sound of it being ripped from the wall, the wadding of paper, followed by more whimpering, then the water running, and what could have been a groan of relief. Then the door to the restroom being swung open and slammed shut.

I waited a good thirty seconds before opening the door to my stall. Very carefully, leading with my gun, I eased the door open and looked around. It was now dead silent in the bathroom. I saw a trail of blood and, on opening the door a little farther, saw that it led from the other stall to the sink. I stepped out watchfully and saw that there was a pile of wet, bloody paper towels on the floor next to the dispenser, and even more bloody sheets in the sink, where the faucet was still running. I moved to the restroom door and inched it open. I couldn't see anything, except more blood, so I went outside.

I followed a trail of red goo leading from the door to the bathroom, around the back of the convenience store, and into the desert.

A white pick-up truck in need of a new muffler came roaring down the road and skidded into the parking lot. There were two guys in front and two guys in the back, and they all jumped out at once, hooting and hollering. They were all carrying shotguns. I slid my .38 into the back of my pants. I figured I didn't need to show anybody I had it until I really needed it.

"Hey, did you see something weird come by here?" one of them asked. I could smell whiskey on his breath, or at least coming from somewhere.

"What do you mean weird?" I asked.

"What do I mean weird? Something unusual. We were out hunting, and I swear to God we saw something about seven feet tall with a big, pointed head squatting down next to a coyote and it was feasting on it like it was Thanksgiving dinner. We shot at it. I think I hit it, but it moved off into the desert, heading this way." He paused and stared at me for a few moments. Exasperated, he asked, "Have you seen anyone or anything fitting that description, pardner?"

"Can't say as I have," I said. After all, that was the truth. I hadn't seen him.

They hopped back into their pick-up and drove farther down the road. A couple of minutes later, I saw it. A purple meteor. Only it wasn't heading toward earth—it was heading up into the sky. I only hoped it was my friend from the next stall finding somewhere safe to go.

# Translove Airlines
## Marc Harshman


They were real clouds.
They were boring clouds.
We were in them.
We were bored.
We were expecting a *quid pro quo*
            ala Constable or Turner—we were
            over the Midlands, weren't we?
And where was the Meissen china,
            the vintage Narcissus tea?
And weren't we going first-class for the view?
And for that we needed movies,
            movement, movie-ment, at least,
            not modern art, not all this white,
            not Olson's open field, not a tabula rasa
            of static snow, not these clouds.
We wanted moving color,
            we wanted to be
            *flying in a green light,*
            Technicolor, bright
            pigments of every hue but . . .


After they threw us out they wrote
            in the pilot's log that
            we were thrown
            into a perfectly blue sky
            amidst twenty black clouds
            and we were of three faces
            each as white as a sheet.

*Italicized lines from "Thirteen Ways of Looking at a Blackbird," Wallace Stevens.*

# A Village Near the Border

Marc Harshman

I read about black-backed gulls
      in the Gulf of Bothnia
      skating under mica-flecked stars
      in the heavy, Swedish winters.
The ghost of a large doe floats
      down my bank, shimmering
      in a confluence of dreams and sirens.
Telepathic, she crosses a frontier
      outside my window and,
      with no passport to show,
      does so with a diffident pride.
I salute, and realize how very close
      reality has come to kiss
      my fingertips with something like blessing.
If only the words could pause
      long enough for the atoms
      catapulting head over heels
      within me to abate,
      I might quit trying so hard
      to keep all the lights on
      in this village of gray matter
      and let the tumble-race
      passing for thought subside,
      and with what truth then remains,
      hope you'll believe me
      when I say we're nearing
      that border where all will be revealed.

# The Woodcutter: A Conversation with Sheldon Russell

*Lowestoft Chronicle*

Dr. Sheldon Russell
(Photography: Bob Bozarth/Bozarth Photography, Guthrie, OK)

A recipient of two Oklahoma Book Awards for Fiction, The Langum Project for Historical Literature, The Official Centennial Project for literature in Oklahoma, praise from the *New York Times* for his Hook Runyon mysteries, and starred reviews by *Booklist* and *Publishers Weekly*, Sheldon Russell holds an impressive fiction writer's resume. In 2001, his stirring novel, *Requiem at Dawn*, was a finalist for the Western Writers of America's Spur Award, and *The Insane Train*, the second book in his acclaimed series featuring a one-armed railroad detective living in a caboose, was selected by *Publishers Weekly* as one of the six best mysteries of 2010.

*Lowestoft Chronicle* flagged down Russell and invited him to discuss the inspiration behind some of his literary work and give an update on the Hook Runyon series.

**Lowestoft Chronicle (LC):** Over the years, you've written suspense novels, tales of the Oklahoma Land Rush and the American frontier, postwar mysteries, and a fictional account of Francisco Vázquez Coronado's 1540s North American expedition. In *A Forgotten Evil*, you spirit the reader to the post-Civil War period where bloody skirmishes rage between the U.S. Army and Native American Indians. What drew you to this period? Am I right in thinking that this was a novel, initially titled *The Woodcutter*, that you started work on sometime prior to 2013?

**Sheldon Russell (SR):** Yes, this book began its life as *The Woodcutter*. I worked on it for several years and through several revisions, finally changing the title to *A Forgotten Evil*. Ironically, the first question one of my readers asked was why I didn't title it *The Woodcutter*. Go figure? I admit to still rather liking the first title.

My inspiration for this book came about when my wife and I made a weekend trip to the Washita Battlefield National Historic Site, a couple of hours from where we live. It is a silent and sad place in the Antelope Hills area of Oklahoma, haunted still by the tragic deaths of so many people. I was moved.

We made other trips to a number of forts in Kansas. I wanted to know the details of that life. What did their blacksmith shops look like? What tools did they use? What did they sell at the Sutler's store? What kind of discipline was doled out to the common soldier? Kansas has done a remarkable job of keeping these forts in pristine condition. They had exactly what I was needing.

**LC:** In this novel, you cast light on the atrocities perpetrated at the Battle of Washita River, a controversial yet little discussed battle. What was your motivation for writing this book? What misconceptions do you think you held before you started your research?

**SR:** To look out over that valley is to know that it is a sacred place and that what happened there should never be forgotten. I wanted to do my part in keeping the memory alive. I make no claim to be a historian, but I do know what being lost on the prairie must feel like, what skills are necessary to survive, what the human spirit can endure if necessary. It is one thing to know the history of an event, quite another to know a moment. It's not enough for readers to know that people died in this place. They must grieve for it as well.

I think my biggest misconception was that I hadn't fully realized to what lengths the Indians had gone to in order to avoid this confrontation. It was not to be.

**LC:** Why did you choose the young Ohioan woodcutter, Caleb Justin, as the narrator rather than, say, the hopeful Army recruit, Joshua Hart?

**SR:** I taught at the University of Louisville, back in the day, and had some memorable experiences on the Belle of Louisville and the Ohio River that I thought I could bring to bear on the story. Caleb, not unlike myself as a boy, lives remote and mostly in his head. He is serious and sensitive, perhaps to a fault, but I thought he was best able to see all sides of the story. While I enjoyed Joshua's sense of humor and adventure, he was less equipped intellectually and emotionally to step outside of his own culture and to see how marvelously adept the Cheyenne were in their environment. I admit to enjoying the banter between Caleb and Joshua, but I do have to exercise discretion with this aspect of their relationship. I'm capable of carrying it too far.

**LC:** What I enjoyed most about this story is Caleb's frightening yet fascinating experiences living with the Cheyenne tribe and his relationship with his captor, the imposing Indian warrior Little River, who becomes his mentor. Though fierce and remorseless, Little River is also benevolent, considerate, and capable of humor. Was it at all challenging depicting him and giving him an authentic voice? Is he pure fiction or based on a real-life Cheyenne warrior?

**SR:** It's not based directly on any historical character but rather on character itself. I wanted an evolving relationship between Caleb and Little River, one based on respect and trust. I wanted the reader to know Little River as a person who lived a full and satisfying life and to appreciate his intelligence and his skills. The relationship between him and Caleb does not mature completely until that moment that they can safely joke with each other. We do not joke with our enemies. By definition, joking with someone requires a dissipation of anxiety and defensiveness.

**LC:** The story takes some unexpected turns with, essentially, three key characters affecting the course of Caleb's life—Joshua, Little River, and Joan Monnet, the daughter of a wealthy industrialist. How did you go about structuring this novel? Did the narrative arc change as these characters developed?

**SR:** This book was a bit different for me from the beginning, my approach to writing it, that is. I had a pretty clear vision of where I was going from the outset. I wanted a journey. I wanted adolescent boys stepping out on their own for the first time. I wanted a courageous woman. It was about time for that.

**LC:** How did your approach to this book differ from prior books? I think in our previous interview, you said: "To me, all stories are journeys. Once I know what the journey is, I can then outline each chapter before I write it, some of it little more than brainstorming." Did this book follow that method?

**SR:** It's not always clear to me how my writing might change from one book to another. I had spent considerable time and effort over the years writing my Hook Runyon Mystery Series, where plot was necessarily a major consideration. With this project, the plot had already been written in the history books. My job was to bring to life the characters, the times, and especially the emotions, a process largely driven by the subconscious, I suspect. The results can sometimes be revelatory but also exhausting.

**LC:** "I write from beginning to end, often rewriting the first chapter after I'm finished," you once said. *A Forgotten Evil* has a particularly poignant opening, with the main protagonist burying his father. Did you always intend to begin the narrative this way?

**SR:** I wrote the chapter about Caleb's father right out of the chute and didn't change it. My own father, who lived to be a hundred, had only recently died. When a boy or man loses his father, he necessarily steps up to the grave himself. It's an uneasy feeling. Suddenly, he must make his own decisions and mistakes and face the world on its terms. I guess those feelings were mine at the time I started this book, and they just came out, as they are sometimes wont to do. Still, they are universal feelings, I think, and something most of us have experienced at one point or the other.

**LC:** Your fiction is routinely imbued with historical detail, suspenseful passages, and elegant prose. This novel is notable for its wonderfully vivid descriptions of war-ravaged prairie landscapes, vicious battles, Caleb's harsh, alienated existence, and the hardships faced by those trying to evade capture and survive in the wilderness. Did you make a conscious effort to embroider the language and give the manuscript a rich, lyrical beauty? Have you always had a propensity for literary fiction? Who would you say are your biggest literary influences?

**SR:** Once started on this book, I wrote with abandon, less editing, and less censoring from the outset. I wanted an ending that would not be easily forgotten, and I knew where and how that would come about. If I thought it, I wrote it, which resulted in revealing my penchant for introductory adverbial clauses. But, being more willing to write the bad stuff allowed me to write the good stuff as well, I think. Thank goodness for the editing process.

I fell in love with Mark Twain's work when I was a kid. Who doesn't? Somewhere along the line, I decided that's what I wanted to do, and I guess most writers fancy themselves as literary at some point. I went on to do graduate work in English, became fascinated with American novelists, primarily Hemingway, Steinbeck, and Fitzgerald. Over the years, my reading has expanded to include favorites such as Conroy, Frazier, MacDonald, and many others. I have no doubt that I've tried to emulate them all. Now, I just try to tell the best story that I can. I don't get too far from my own experiences, and I have become better at dealing with rejection. My work habits are pretty good, and I've had some competent editors to help me out along the way. It's been a satisfying life. No regrets.

**LC:** In our previous interview, you mentioned you had completed a rough draft of *Evil Rides A Train*, the next Hook Runyon mystery, and were writing an autobiographical novel, tentatively titled *A Particular Madness*. Are these two books now complete? What other fiction projects are you currently working on?

**SR:** I've completed two additional Hook Runyon mysteries at this point, *Evil Rides a Train* and *Touch of Rage*. Both are in the pipeline for publication. *A Particular Madness* is currently under consideration. Other manuscripts being considered include *Time and Again*, a novel based on the Burnham Site, a recent archeological discovery near where I live that suggests that man inhabited North America much earlier than thought. And I have yet another being read, *Cougar Mountain*, about a small-town doctor in the Southwest who, through eugenics, breeds a champion football team. Yes, I know, but King gets by with it. I've only recently, thirty thousand words or so, embarked on a new mystery I'm calling *Willful Obsessions*, about the estate sales business and the strange happenings that can be uncovered in all that stuff we leave behind.

# Contributors

Before the poetry bug struck her, **Linda Ankrah-Dove** was privileged to work as an economist and sociologist in developing countries all over the world. A decade ago, she founded First Monday Poets in her new home in the Shenandoah Valley of Virginia, and more recently, gained her cross-genre MFA in poetry. Her early poetry, 2007-2018, featured in her *Borrowed Glint of Jade*, and she has also published poems in the *Virginia Literary Review*, *EchoWorld*, several Bridgewater International festival anthologies, *MonthstoYears*, *PoetryXHunger*, DC Trending, and the anthology, *Written in Arlington*. Her poem won first prize in the 2021 Shenandoah Green Earth Day Poetry Contest.

**Robert Beveridge** makes noise (xterminal.bandcamp.com) and writes poetry in Akron, OH. Recent appearances in *Collective Unrest*, *Cough Syrup Magazine*, and *Blood & Bourbon*, among others.

**Jeff Burt** lives in Santa Cruz County, California. He has contributed work to *Gold Man Review*, *Per Contra*, *Bird's Thumb*, and *Lowestoft Chronicle*.

**DeWitt Clinton** taught English, Creative Writing, and World of Ideas courses for over 30 years at the University of Wisconsin—Whitewater. His earlier collections of poetry include *The Conquistador Dog Texts, The Coyot. Inca Texts*, (New Rivers Press), *At the End of the War* (Kelsay Books, 2018), *By A Lake Near A Moon: Fishing with the Chinese Masters* (Is A Rose Press, 2020), and *Hello There* (Word Tech Communications, 2021). He lives in the Village of Shorewood, just across the street from Milwaukee.

**DAH** is a multiple Pushcart Prize and Best Of The Net

nominee and the author of nine books of poetry. He lives in Berkeley, California, where he is simultaneously working on his tenth poetry collection and his first collection of short fiction. DAH's fourth book, *The Translator*, was nominated for the Pulitzer Prize by publisher Dustin Pickering of Transcendent Zero Press. https://dahlusion.wordpress.com/

**Rob Dinsmoor**, a frequent contributor to *Lowestoft Chronicle*, has published three memoirs: *Tales of the Troupe, The Yoga Divas and Other Stories*, and *You Can Leave Anytime*. His short story collection, *Toxic Cookout*, was published by Big Table Publishing.

**Mary Donaldson-Evans**' creative work has been published by the *Lowestoft Chronicle, Boomer Lit Magazine, The Literary Hatchet, The Metaworker Literary Magazine*, and *Spank the Carp*, among others. Her book, *Behind the Lines: A Soldier, his Family and the 10th Mountain Division*, was published by Austin-Macauley Publishers, London. She can be reached at marydonevans@gmail.com.

**Catherine Dowling** was born in Ireland and has divided her life between the United States and her home country. She has a Masters in History from the University of Montana and has worked hard to create a chequered resume that includes waitressing, quality assurance, teaching, and psychotherapy as well as writing. She has published two books: *Racial Awareness* (Llewellyn Worldwide), and *Rebirthing and Breathwork* (Piatkus, UK). Her articles have appeared in *Oneing, r.kv.r.y. Quarterly Literary Journal, Positive Health, Inside Out, Lowestoft Chronicle, Montana Mouthful* and more. They can be found at http://www.catherinedowling.com. She has lived in New York, Montana, California, and New Mexico but currently resides in Ireland.

**Tim Frank**'s short stories have been published in *Bourbon Penn, Eunoia Review, Menacing Hedge, Maudlin House*, and elsewhere. He is the associate fiction editor for *Able Muse Literary Journal*.

**Abby Frucht** is the author of two story collections, *Fruit of the Month* and *The Bell at the End of a Rope*, and five novels, *Snap*, *Licorice*, *Are You Mine?*, *Life Before Death*, and *Polly's Ghost*. She is a member of the faculty at the Vermont College of Fine Arts, and lives in Oshkosh, Wisconsin.

**James Gallant** was the winner of 2019 Schaffner Press Prize for music-in-literature for his story collection, *La Leona, and Other Guitar Stories*, published in 2020. *Fortnightly Review* (UK) published in 2018 in its Odd Volumes series a collection of his essays and short fiction, *Verisimilitudes: Essays and Approximations*.

**Bruce Harris** writes crime and mystery stories. His baseball murder mystery, *Death in the Dugout*, is available on Amazon.

**Marc Harshman**'s *Woman in Red Anorak*, won the Blue Lynx Poetry Prize and was published in 2018 by Lynx House/ University of Washington Press. His fourteenth children's book, *Fallingwater*, co-authored with Anna Smucker, was published by Roaring Brook/Macmillan in 2017. He is also co-winner of the 2019 Allen Ginsberg Poetry Award. Poems have been anthologized by Kent State University, the University of Iowa, University of Georgia, and the University of Arizona. He is the seventh poet laureate of West Virginia.

**Jacqueline Jules** is the author of three chapbooks: *Field Trip to the Museum* (Finishing Line Press), *Stronger Than Cleopatra* (ELJ Publications), and *Itzhak Perlman's Broken String*, winner of the 2016 Helen Kay Chapbook Prize from Evening Street Press. Her work has appeared in over 100 publications, including *Lowestoft Chronicle*, *The Paterson Literary Review*, *Cider Press Review*, *Potomac Review*, *Inkwell*, *Hospital Drive*, and *Imitation Fruit*. Visit her online at https://metaphoricaltruths. blogspot.com/

**Nicholas Litchfield** is the author of the suspense novel *Swampjack Virus* and editor of ten literary anthologies. His stories, essays, and book reviews appear in many magazines and newspapers, including *BULL: Men's Fiction*, *Shotgun Honey*, *Daily Press*, and *The Virginian-Pilot*. He has also contributed introductions to numerous books, including thirteen Stark House Press reprints of long-forgotten noir and mystery novels. Formerly a book critic for the *Lancashire Post*, syndicated to twenty-five newspapers across the U.K., he now writes for *Publishers Weekly* and regularly contributes to the *Colorado Review*. You can find him online at nicholaslitchfield.com.

**Richard Luftig** is a former professor of educational psychology and special education at Miami University in Ohio, now residing in California. His poems and stories have appeared in numerous literary journals in the United States (including *Lowestoft Chronicle*) and internationally in the United Kingdom, Canada, Australia, Europe, and Asia. Two of his poems recently appeared in *Realms of the Mothers: The First Decade of Dos Madres Press*. His most recent book of poems, *A Grammar for Snow*, was published by Unsolicited Press.

**Robert Mangeot** lives in Franklin, Tennessee with his wife and cats. His short fiction appears here and there, including *Alfred Hitchcock's Mystery Magazine*, *The Forge Literary Magazine*, *Lowestoft Chronicle*, *Mystery Writers of America Presents Ice Cold: Tales of Intrigue from the Cold War*, the Anthony-winning *Murder Under the Oaks*, and *The Oddville Press*. When not doing any of that, he can be found wandering the snack food aisles of America or France.

**George Moore**'s poetry has appeared in *The Atlantic*, *Poetry*, *North American Review*, *Colorado Review*, *Orion*, and *Stand*. He has published six collections, the most recent of which are *Children's Drawings of the Universe* (Salmon Poetry 2015) and *Saint Agnes Outside the Walls* (FurureCycle 2016). He is a seven-time Pushcart Prize nominee and a finalist for The National Poetry Series. His work has been shortlisted for the Bailieborough Poetry Prize and long-listed for the Gregory O'Donoghue and Ginkgo Poetry Prizes. After a career at the University of Colorado, Boulder, he lives with his wife, a Canadian poet, on the south shore of Nova Scotia.

**James B. Nicola** is the author of six collections of poetry: *Manhattan Plaza*, *Stage to Page*, *Wind in the Cave*, *Out of Nothing: Poems of Art and Artists*, *Quickening: Poems from Before and Beyond* (2019), and *Fires of Heaven: Poems of Faith and Sense* (2021). His theater career culminated in the nonfiction book *Playing the Audience: The Practical Guide to Live Performance*, which won a Choice award.

Dr. **Sheldon Russell** retired as Professor Emeritus from the University of Central Oklahoma in 2000. He has had thirteen novels published: *Empire*, a suspense novel; two historic frontier novels, *The Savage Trail* and *Requiem at Dawn*; *Dreams to Dust: A Tale of the Oklahoma Land Rush*; *The Dig: In Search of Coronado's Treasure*; *A Forgotten Evil*; *Time and Again*; *A Particular Madness*; and the Hook Runyon mystery series (*The Yard Dog*, *The Insane Train*, *Dead Man's Tunnel*, *The Hanging of Samuel Ash*, and *The Bridge Troll Murders*). He and his wife currently reside on their home ranch in northwestern Oklahoma, where they both work daily at their respective crafts.

**Robert Wexelblatt** is a professor of humanities at Boston University's College of General Studies. He has published eight collections of short stories; two books of essays; two short novels; two books of poems; stories, essays, and poems in a variety of journals, and a novel awarded the Indie Book Awards first prize for fiction.

# Copyright Notes

## Bon Voyage!

# Other Places

### Edited by Nicholas Litchfield

"In the age of tweets and sound bites, it's heartening to read *Other Places*, a publication celebrating the power and beauty of a story well told."
—Sheldon Russell, author of the Hook Runyon Mystery series

"*Other Places*, a mouth-watering feast of short stories, poems, narrative non-fiction, and in-depth interviews, is the latest anthology from the much-admired *Lowestoft Chronicle*, an eclectic and innovative online journal. Packed into the pages are stories to entice, enthral, and entertain. Litchfield also serves up a tasty blend of pleasing and deftly prepared poems. And if you still aren't sated by this literary banquet, tuck into Litchfield's incisive and enlightening interviews with three critically acclaimed, multitalented writers."
—Pam Norfolk, *Wigan Evening Post*

"I really loved the latest anthology from Lowestoft, *Other Places*. It's a brilliant, savory, sharp, amusing and varied taste of my favorite magazine, *Lowestoft Chronicle*. I'm delighted that a place exists for this kind of travel writing—if that's a term for it. And it's not a good one. This is just great writing about place, ranging from the spirit of place to the human spirit. Go anywhere with Lowestoft. And enjoy the trip."
—Jay Parini, internationally bestselling author of *The Passages of H.M.*

"*Other Places* is the usual delightful mix of stories, poems, author interviews, and non-fiction gleaned from the pages of the *Lowestoft Chronicle*, the only literary magazine I read on a regular basis. Always entertaining and insightful, *Other Places* is well worth your time, whether you're a veteran traveler or a hermit like me!"
—James Reasoner, *Rough Edges*

"Armchair travelers, rejoice! Editor Nicholas Litchfield has released *Lowestoft Chronicle*'s anthology for summer 2015, *Other Places*. Filled with fiction, nonfiction and poetry about travel and destinations, the book brings the far corners of the world to the reader's armchair. The stories and poems vary in tone from dead serious to delightful whimsy, offering something for every taste. Humor, adventure and mystery share the pages with intriguing result."
—Mary Beth Magee, *Examiner.com*

"Sick of fly-by journalism and travel dilettantes? The antidote is *Lowestoft Chronicle*'s most recent anthology, *Other Places*—a collection of essays, stories, and poetry devoted to the in-depth experience of culture. Whether humorous, touching, or revelatory, these expertly curated pieces throw you in contact with the real."
—Scott Dominic Carpenter, author of *Theory of Remainders*

**To order, visit www.lowestoftchronicle.com**

# Grand Departures

Edited by Nicholas Litchfield
Foreword by Robert Garner McBrearty

"The stories, poems, and essays in Nicholas Litchfield's latest anthology, *Grand Departures*, are haunting, idiosyncratic, and unexpected, like the true delights of travel."
—Ivy Goodman, award-winning author of *Heart Failure*

"A must-have collection of travelers' delights and demons."
—Nancy Caronia, contributor to *Somewhere, Sometime* and co-editor of *Personal Effects*

"An impressive collection of travel works that sweeps the reader across the globe."
—Dorene O'Brien, award-winning author of *Voices of the Lost and Found*

"It is fun, edgy at times, international in its scope. It surprises. The work is a blend of the serious and the comical, dark shades, light shades, and as I said, ever surprising."
—Robert Garner McBrearty, author of *The Western Lonesome Society*

# Invigorating Passages

Edited by Nicholas Litchfield
Foreword by Matthew P. Mayo

"A powerful literary passport—this adventurous anthology is all stamped up with exciting travel-themed writing. With humor, darkness, and charm, its lively prose and poetry will drop you into memorable physical and psychological landscapes. Pack your bags!"
—Joseph Scapellato, acclaimed author of *Big Lonesome*

"A wonderful collection from a fine literary journal. Fine writing that stirs the imagination, often amuses and always entertains."
—Dietrich Kalteis, award-winning author of *Ride the Lightning*

"*Invigorating Passages* delivers on all counts, hits on all cylinders too. The writing is skilled, the choices rich, the passages manifold, and the invigoration unfailing."
—Robert Wexelblatt, award-winning author of *Zublinka Among Women*

"*Invigorating Passages* is a rare and dynamic literary collection which grabs readers firmly and sweeps them away to strange and exhilarating places, presenting intriguing situations, colourful characters, and making us yearn to strap on the backpack and go exploring."
—Pam Norfolk, *Lancashire Post*

To order, visit www.lowestoftchronicle.com